SLEEP OF DEATH

by the same author

DEATH OF A WEDDING GUEST
NURSERY TEA AND POISON
KILLING WITH KINDNESS
DEATH OF A HEAVENLY TWIN
DEATH AND THE DUTIFUL DAUGHTER
MURDER IN MIMICRY
SCARED TO DEATH
MURDER BY PROXY
DEATH IN THE ROUND
THE MEN IN HER DEATH
HOLLOW VENGEANCE

SLEEP OF DEATH

Anne Morice

ST. MARTIN'S PRESS
NEW YORK

Library of Congress Cataloging in Publication Data

Morice, Anne.
    Sleep of death.

    I. Title.
PR6063.0743S6   1983   823'.914   82-17023
ISBN 0-312-72863-8

First published in Great Britain by Macmillan London Ltd.

First U.S. Edition
10 9 8 7 6 5 4 3 2 1

CHAPTER ONE

I

The opening night of *Elders and Betters*, a comedy based on the theory that a sixth sense, backed up by a lifetime's experience, is worth more than the other five put together, had been set for Thursday, 20th May, but Robin told me he would prefer to see it either at a preview or at a later performance, whichever suited me best.

He does not much care for the overheated atmosphere of first nights and furthermore his superiors at Scotland Yard have perfected the art of discovering some urgent and essential business for him on those rare evenings which he has set aside for private engagements. In accordance with some law, which I do not believe has yet been researched and identified, the further ahead the private engagement has been made, the shorter the notice allowed to him for its cancellation. Aware that to be the cause of leaving two vacant seats in the fifth row of the stalls on the opening night would put him in bad odour with the management and company, he preferred to play safe and, since this is a game you can't win, to spend the evening alone and at home, in front of the television set.

'Then you had better settle for the first preview,' I told him, 'which is today week. For one thing, I'll be able to hear in advance how much you enjoyed it and how wonderful I was, which is bound to boost my morale, whether I believe you or not. For another . . .'

'Oh, do we need another?'

'I'm afraid we're stuck with it. I have a nasty feeling that the first night could also be the last, and you might miss it altogether.'

'Then shouldn't I make it the second preview? You're bound to last as long as that and it would give me a better chance to catch you at your peak.'

'Yes, it would, but the second preview is not for the likes of you, who have to work. It takes place on Thursday afternoon; a few hours before the official opening, in fact.'

'That's punishing yourselves a bit, isn't it?'

'Yes, and just about all we needed. As I've told you more times than you probably care to remember, it's not a bad play, quite well constructed and funny, but we've been dogged from the start by such rotten luck. No less than two actors being struck down by near fatal diseases half way through rehearsals must be some kind of a record and it's gone on like that ever since. If we'd been doing a play about a Scotsman who had a strange encounter with three witches, the going couldn't have been rougher.'

'So why throw in an afternoon preview, to make it rougher still?'

'It seems that Oliver had no choice. It now turns out that we clash with the opening of the *Candida* revival, which happens to be a rather more prestigious production, with rather bigger star names, so it was a question of getting the press to a special preview, or not getting them at all.'

'Rather inefficient of him not to have discovered this before, wasn't it?'

'Well, he is new to the game, in the sense of being out on his own for the first time, but this wasn't his fault. Owing to a succession of flops, the Coronet became vacant unexpectedly and the *Candida* lot have cut short their tour and are coming in a week earlier than planned. At least, that's what I heard and, as far as I'm concerned, it's just one more instance of the rotten luck which has beset us all the way through. Shall I pour you some coffee?'

'I'd love it, but my time's up. See you some time this evening! I take it you'll be rehearsing all the hours your union will allow?'

'Oh, you bet! Unless the roof falls in, which is about the only disaster we've so far been spared.'

'Cheer up! Things usually turn out better than you expect.'

'If not worse,' I remarked gloomily, thinking of the long, hard and probably unrewarding day ahead.

There was a flight of stone steps from ground level up to the dressing rooms and that morning I had to take them very slowly because, just ahead of me and making heavy weather of it, was old Philip Mickleton, K.B.E., our recently recruited star performer. I was careful to give him a good start and to match my pace with his, because one of his few faculties which remained in good trim was his hearing and it seemed likely that, if he were to turn round to see which porpoise was close behind him, he would lose his balance, topple over and send us both hurtling to the bottom.

In fact, it struck me that he was distinctly more tottery than he had been the day before and the sight of his decrepit old figure brought back all the dismal forebodings which my early morning walk through the Park had done much to dispel, for the truth was that at least half the misfortunes which I had been moaning about to Robin could be laid at the door of Sir Philip Mickleton.

He had received his knighthood in the previous year's Birthday Honours, causing bafflement to a number of people, since he was only a moderately celebrated actor, had never taken on any of the great classical roles and was more renowned for his vanity and irascible temper than for his contribution either to charity or the performing arts. His professional activities over the past few years had been confined mainly to cameo film parts and voice-overs for television commercials.

Various explanations had been put forward for the honour which had been so unexpectedly conferred on him, the most popular being that someone in the Civil Service had goofed. It was a widely held belief in the profession that the man whose job it was to notify the intended recipients had mixed him up with another Philip Mickleton and the real nominee, a successful and influential industrialist based in Edinburgh.

In the nature of things, almost everyone in the company had come into contact with him at one time or another, but I alone could claim the dubious distinction of a special relationship. This had stemmed from the fact that, for a brief period during her early married life, he had been one of my mother's most ardent, persistent and unsnubbable admirers and, at about the time when I was four or five years old, had been a frequent visitor at our house, often seeking to curry favour with the chatelaine by plying me with unsuitable toys and treats. Nowadays it amused him to pretend that this had created a unique bond, almost a blood relationship one might have supposed, which could never now be severed.

Ironically enough, the decline into comparative obscurity had eventually worked in his favour, because when Freddie Marloe, who had been engaged for the leading role of the grandfather, was snatched from our midst by a thrombosis, during the third week of rehearsals, Philip had turned out to be one of the very few actors of suitable age and style who was immediately available to take over. At the time, though, the replacement had not been made without certain misgivings and these had increased with every day that passed. However, as I had explained to Robin, Oliver Welles, who was presenting the play, and Tim McCartney, our director, had really had no choice. It was Oliver's very first West End venture, after setting up in management on his own, and his whole future, not to mention some heavy financial backing, was at stake. The play, when it opened, might flounder or succeed, its outcome being one which no one could ever predict, but in the meantime the first essential was to stick as rigidly as circumstances would allow to the schedule which

8

had been laid down.

Aware of this and also of the unfavourable circumstances into which Philip had been thrown, with the rest of us all now getting well into our parts and he having had no opportunity for more than a single reading of the script, every allowance had been made. The entire company had striven like maniacs to make things as easy as possible for him and, at first, the response had not been discouraging. He had certainly got the portrayal of old age, with its occasional lapses into near senility, to perfection. Disillusionment had only begun to set in when it gradually became clear that this had little to do with acting, but was merely the manifestation of his own physical and mental condition. At the end of three weeks he was almost as shaky over his lines as he had been at the start and there were still worse trials than that.

There was a scene in the first act, for instance, between the old man and his grandson, which gradually developed into an impassioned monologue and plea for support and understanding on the part of the boy, brought to an end by my own entrance, in the role of the boy's sister, who instantly and smugly drew his attention to the fact that his grandfather was fast asleep. Twice, so far, during rehearsals, it had turned out that Philip actually was fast asleep, which was perfectly all right for him, since a display of fluster and incoherence was quite appropriate when he was shaken awake by the young people, but not so good for the young people themselves, who waited in vain for their cues.

Hardly a day had passed since then without some such incident to rock us back on our heels and, since there is no more fertile breeding ground for bad luck than a patch where a lot of it has sprung up already, it was not to be wondered at that pessimism was now becoming rampant. It had obviously taken a hold on Oliver too and we noticed with growing dismay that he was becoming daily more elusive and inaccessible, ever more inclined to leave administrative problems to his inexperienced junior partner, Benjamin Hartman, whose only, though far from negligible asset was a father whose address book was stuffed with the names of people with money to burn, a surprising number of whom were not averse to seeing some of it go up in smoke in the entertainment business.

He was not a bad young man either, this Benjie, full of enthusiasm, eager to please and quite unashamedly stage struck. There could be no question that he had bought his way into the theatre through a genuine love of it, which was a mark in his favour, specially as the purchase was liable to prove so expensive. On the other hand, he was rather too apt to throw his weight about, oblivious of the fact that his weight, measured in terms of knowledge and experience, was far too light to stand up to such treatment.

These, among other depressing reflections, had been passing through my mind as I plodded slowly upstairs and, when Philip was safely at the top and had turned left down the corridor towards his dressing room, which was in the opposite direction to my own, I bounded up the last of them, sped along to the right and then, with my hand on the doorknob, changed course and continued on to the room next to it. The door was half open, a sure sign that the occupant was inside and in a mood for visitors and, since twenty minutes remained before the rehearsal call, I decided that I could do worse than spend them catching up with developments in the dramatic life of my old friend, Clarissa Jones.

II

She had not been born Clarissa Jones, but had adopted the name when setting out to become an actress, on the grounds that her real one, which was Charity Jenkins was unsuitable for the stage, although I could never see why, since one seemed to have as good a ring about it as the other. From her admission that she had been tempted at one time to call herself Jezebel Harlett, I concluded that it had most likely been a gesture of revolt against her very strict Low Church upbringing. Until she walked out of it and came to London at the age of seventeen, she had spent all her life in a shabby, draughty and hideously uncomfortable Victorian parsonage, being nagged into stupors by her parents and two elder sisters, who were called Prudence and Faith.

Thereafter, change of nomenclature had tended to become a habit and she had already swept through two marriages, not to mention numerous other liaisons, with the speed of a hurricane rushing down the east coast of America. She may well have been unique among drama students in having paid her final year's fees out of the alimony she received from her first husband.

She had recently acquired what she called a new steady, although firmly denying that she had any intention of marrying him and, with such a rapid turnover always on the go, it was sometimes quite hard to remember the name of the current *amour*. I often suspected that Clarrie may also have experienced a little difficultly here. It was her invariable practice to address him simply as "Darling" or "my angel", while referring to him in his absence in such vague terms as "the old man", or "that brute".

She and I had first met at a very early stage in our careers, when we were playing in rep. in the Midlands and, despite some marked differences in tastes and temperaments, had remained friends, in a detached and off-hand way, ever since. In fact, in the early days, before the disasters began to rain down, we had both regarded it as a propitious omen that we should have teamed up again in this exciting new production.

The joke was that she had been cast as the placid, besotted, somewhat bovine granddaughter, married to an excessively tiresome man, in whom she could see no fault at all, whereas I played the neurotic, discontented one, forever knocking back whisky and doing her utmost to gum things up for the rest of the family.

Nevertheless, so far as Clarrie was concerned, I could see why the parts had been doled out in this way, for there was often something sleepy in her expression and this, combined with her luxuriant dark hair, creamy complexion and tendency to plumpness, produced an overall effect of complaisant serenity, verging on indolence. It was deceptive, however, because she was fiery and volatile by nature, highly extroverted and capable on occasions of extreme ruthlessness. There was certainly nothing placid about her mood that morning, although the rage and self-pity were only indirectly connected with our professional problems.

'You're never going to believe me when I tell you what that rotten imbecile has gone and done now,' she informed me.

'Which rotten imbecile? Pete?'

'That's the one.'

'What has he done now?'

'Been chatting up her ladyship and invited them both over to lunch on Sunday. Did you ever hear of anything so ghoulish?'

Unlike the rotten imbecile, no explanation was required as to who was meant by "her ladyship". She was referring to Dolly Mickleton, Philip's wife, a domineering and self-opinionated woman, only saved from being thoroughly detestable by the pathetic absurdity of her name-dropping snobbery, and who never allowed anyone to forget that she now had a title.

Nor was it necessary to explain why she and Pete were on these chummy terms, for in a sense they were both in the same boat, united in being on the periphery of the action. Pete made a regular practice of collecting Clarrie between and at the end of rehearsal sessions, which inevitably involved a good deal of hanging about at the theatre, whereas Dolly was almost always somewhere on the premises, ready to minister to Philip's every need, to make sure that he took his pills and got every minute of rest that the schedule would allow.

'Never,' I admitted. 'Why do you suppose he would do a thing like that?'

'Devilment, as my poor mother used to say. He's a great little mixer, you know. Show him a flock of pigeons and he'll put the cat in. Other people's hell sends him into hysterics. It'll get him into trouble one of these days, as I'm always telling him. Your sins will find you out, I say. Hope it doesn't happen to you and me too, dear! Well, you're in no danger, I daresay, in your snug little rut.'

'Nor you either, since you broadcast your sins, even as you commit them, and treat the world as your private confessional. It must be a safeguard. But listen, Clarrie, aren't you even more surprised, in a way, that her ladyship accepted?'

'No, I'm not. Stingy brutes, I bet they'd go anywhere for a free meal.'

'Oh, I agree and they probably don't get offered one all that often, but just think what it'll cost them in petrol. Don't they spend all their weekends in that Old Rectory place near Goring?'

'Which happens to be about eight miles from the hilltop cottage where Pete and I spend our weekends.'

'Oh, really? I didn't know.'

'Well, it's pretty crummy, so I don't often invite people and, anyway, come Sunday, I'm usually too exhausted to bother with cooking proper meals, even for my friends. I'm really livid about it, but I suppose I can't exactly tell them not to come?'

'No, I doubt if that would do very much to brighten the atmosphere.'

'Well, in that case . . . listen, Tessa!'

'I'm listening.'

'Why don't you and Robin have mercy on me and come and help out?'

13

'Then you'd be cooking for six people, instead of four.'

'Oh, come on! You know damn well how much difference that would make! Besides, you'd be able to help with the washing-up,' she added, not being without the cunning streak. 'But the main thing is that between us we might be able to keep her ladyship in order. If I have to take her on single-handed, she'll be mopping up the floor with me, passing remarks about chipped plates and paper napkins and saying she hopes I haven't put any onions in the stew because they bring Philip out in a rash. Oh, be a sport, for once in your miserable life!'

'All right, we will, if we can, but I'll have to check with Robin. He may have something on.'

'In that case, nothing to stop you coming on your own,' she replied cheerfully, showing the cunning and ruthless streaks running in harness.

In fact, no proposal could have appealed to me less, because the most blissful thing about Sunday at this period was that it was the one day of the week when I did not have to set eyes on, or allow my mind to dwell very much on, Philip Mickleton, a factor which normally outweighed all other considerations, including the ties of friendship, but when I pointed this out to Clarrie she had reminded me airily that the Lord giveth and the Lord taketh away. I was inclined to agree with her, although my conditional consent had been based on more practical grounds. Her remark about the cottage being in the hills about eight miles north of Goring had suggested that it might not be much further from Roakes Common, one of whose prominent citizens is my cousin, Toby Crichton. He leads a self-centred and reclusive life there, pretending to be hard at work writing plays and just occasionally committing a line or two to paper. He rarely comes to London and also has a phobia about picking up the telephone, all of this making communication uphill work. However, he never seems displeased when Robin and I invite ourselves to Roakes for the weekend and, since it was now some time since we had taken advantage of this, it had struck me that what we had here was an opportunity to repair the omission, while at the same time throwing in a small, heavily solicited favour to my old friend, Clarissa Jones.

CHAPTER TWO

'Are you sure you won't come with us?' I asked for the second time. 'I know Clarrie would be enchanted to see you.'

'No, thank you. I'm another who doesn't much care for chipped plates and paper napkins. I also detest stew, with or without onions, and I'm not mad about Dolly Mickleton either.'

'I didn't know you'd ever met her.'

'It was a long time ago, but the scars have never quite healed. She had a tiny part in the very first play of mine to be put on. It was very tiny indeed, but she managed to wreck it.'

'Neither did I know she'd been on the stage.'

'Very few people do and it is best forgotten. She chose the wrong calling, as she soon realised, and threw it up at the first opportunity, in favour of a rich husband from South Africa.'

'Not Philip, presumably?'

'No, this was twenty years ago. It didn't last any longer than her theatrical venture, but turned out to be a lot more profitable, I understand.'

'What happened to that one?' Robin asked.

'He walked to the top of Table Mountain and jumped off, during the honeymoon as far as I remember. One can't really blame him.'

'All the same, and to be absolutely fair,' I pointed out, 'she does seem to suit Philip pretty well. Naturally, I try to keep out of their way, as far as possible, but they seem to have a very good understanding. They're always together and she guards him like a lioness protecting her favourite cub.'

'Oh well, she must be in her fifties by now. I daresay the years have mellowed her.'

'But you still won't let Tessa persuade you to come?'

'No, thank you. I doubt if they have mellowed her enough for that.'

We arrived late because I had underestimated the distance, although, unlike Robin, I did not blame myself for this. When I had suggested to Clarrie that it was probably not more than ten or twelve miles, she had instantly agreed, giving it as her opinion that it could well be less, although it turned out to be more like fifteen. My only mistake was in failing to grasp that, having almost ensnared us, she would have agreed to anything at all, very likely putting it as low as three or four, rather than give us an excuse to escape; and, in the mild flurry which so often comes from realising that one is running late, we compounded the evil by swooping past that very turning which we had been assured we could not miss.

Not, to all appearances, that it mattered in the least to Clarrie and Pete, who were both lounging around in a relaxed manner on the narrow strip of enclosed verandah at the side of the cottage. There was no smell of burning from the kitchen, nothing to suggest that anything had so far gone into the oven. All the same, if I had allowed Robin to lose still more time, by stopping at a telephone kiosk to announce that we were going to be late, it might at least have brought a grain of comfort to the other guests, who had obviously arrived punctually and were now paying the penalty.

Dolly, who had ornamented herself with dark glasses, a flamboyant silk scarf, printed all over with the maker's name, and a lot of clanking bracelets, was sitting bolt upright on a garden chair, which was quite a feat, since the two squares of canvas which formed the seat and the back had seen better days and now showed signs of parting company with the frame.

Philip was slightly better off in a wooden deck chair but had doubtless added to his wife's discomfort by embarking on a long and involved anecdote concerning a fellow member of his club. We could tell that it had been going on for some time because, after a perfunctory acknowledgement of our arrival, and egged on by bewitching smiles from his hostess, he took it up again, as though there had been no interruption, thereby frustrating Pete's efforts to find out what Robin and I wanted to drink.

He eventually overcame the problem by stationing himself behind Philip and beside the table where the bottles and other impedimenta were set out, holding up one item after another for our acceptance or otherwise, to which we responded with the appropriate nod or shake of the head. It was rather like being in a dream auction sale and provided me with a unique opportunity to study him quite openly for several minutes.

He was a dark-haired, slant-eyed young man, very neat looking and light on his feet and with graceful, expressive movements, which made me wonder if he had been trained as a dancer at some period, although, if so, it cannot have been a serious vocation. One of the few facts I had learnt about him from Clarrie was that he worked in a snobby and expensive antique shop in Sloane Street. He was doing pretty well out of it too, judging by the lavish display on the bar table, although I guessed him to be not more than twenty-five or six.

By the time this business had been completed, Philip had reached the end of his anecdote, whose only point seemed to have been to introduce the names of some illustrious members of his club, and Pete turned his attention to him and Dolly.

'Thank you, but I'm driving,' Dolly said curtly, when offered another drink, but Philip held up his glass with a shaky hand and announced that the same again would suit him. I considered this to be quite untrue, but Pete darted forward like a moth to the flame, took the glass from him and refilled it to the brim with what appeared to be equal parts of gin and tonic. Having done so, he repeated the performance for Clarrie and then draped himself in an elegant pose on the arm of her chair, his left hand clasping the back of her neck, which she did not appear to notice.

Leaning forward and addressing me as though we were alone together in a railway carriage, Dolly subjected me to a 'barrage of questions about Toby, saying what good times they had shared during the run of one of his early plays and how much she regretted that she so seldom saw him nowadays.

Responding to this with about the same degree of realism, I assured her that he regretted it too, but that pressure of work made it hard for him to keep up with old friends. Going off at a tangent, she next asked me whether it was true that his daughter, Ellen, was married to Lord Roxburgh's elder son.

'Quite true,' I admitted, 'but he wasn't a lord when they married and, anyway, it's only a life peerage, so, in any case, I doubt whether that would have influenced her.'

'Oh, I'm well aware of that, my dear, but what a small world, isn't it? Sybil Roxburgh is one of my oldest friends. We sit on several of the same charity committees. No, really, thank you, Pete. Philip and I have both had quite enough and I'm sure Clarrie will be herding us all into lunch before much longer.'

'No special hurry, is there?' Clarrie asked to no-one in particular and in her most languorous voice.

'None whatever, as far as we're concerned,' I assured her. 'Robin doesn't absolutely need to leave for London until about seven.'

'Okay, sarkie, come and help me do something about it, if that's your attitude,' she said, hauling herself upright, which seemed to require quite an effort. 'Sorry it's only cold,' she added to the others, 'but the bloody old stove is on the blink.'

'The sad fact is, Tessa,' she explained, taking my arm as we went into the house, 'I'm ever so slightly squiffy.'

19

'Oh no, really?'

'Yes, really! Mainly your fault, too. Only I don't blame you for that.'

'I'm so glad. What did I do wrong?'

'Got here at a civilised time, is all. We might have guessed Dolly would bitch things up and that's just what she did. They were hammering on the door at twelve-thirty, would you believe? I'd only just stepped out of the bath.'

Despite this, there was evidence to prove that someone had been at work that morning and had also spent a small fortune at the charcuterie, because a substantial buffet lunch was already set out for us in the room between the verandah and kitchen, which served as combined sitting room, hall and dining room. There were not less than a dozen dishes, each covered with a teacloth, and when I raised a few of the corners I saw that we had been provided with an impressive selection of pâtés, pies, salads and cheeses. There were also four opened bottles of claret and two more of the same, unopened, on a side table, which did not bode quite so well.

The furnishings of this room, although ugly in the extreme, had a more solid look about them than those on the verandah. Nearly everything, in fact, looked like a reject from a defunct Edwardian boarding house and I concluded that the function of this tasteless hotchpotch was to provide some light and shade in a life spent principally in the company of expensive and beautiful objects.

'What's the matter with the stove?' I asked.

'Nothing, as far as I know. I just threw that in because I thought she'd turn up her vulgar nose at a cold lunch. She drives me into these sinful falsehoods. And, in case I forgot to mention it, I'm a bit squiffy and liable to say anything at all, so take no notice.'

'And not the only one, I'm afraid. Philip's looking decidedly glazed.'

'Yes, I know, but, as he's slightly less boring drunk than

sober, who cares? Would you be most terribly kind and make the salad dressing? I've put all the ingredients out on the draining board, but the operation itself requires a cool head and steady hand, neither of which I possess at this particular moment in time.'

She was certainly going out of her way to draw attention to her inebriacy, although in fact I could see little real evidence of it, her speech and movements appearing to be perfectly under control. I concluded that it was a pose, deliberately adopted to provide herself with an excuse in advance, in the event of becoming unable to resist the urge to break into yawns or open rudeness.

The sink was filled with long-stemmed pink roses, many of which had drooped and died while still in the bud stage, immersed up to their dislocated necks in water. In reply to my enquiry, she told me that his godliness had brought them.

'Oliver?'

'Don't sound so surprised. He used to fancy me once upon a time, you know. Wanted to push it to the limits too, until I explained about the other fella in my life. Whereupon he retired with a gentlemanly bow.'

'And is he now coming out of retirement, bearing gifts?'

'No, he was on his way to talk some business with his junior partner, the red-head, who is spending the weekend with his parents in their Cotswold Manor. I think the roses were a bait and he was hoping to be invited to stay on for lunch. He would have too, if that donkey hadn't blown it.'

'How did he do that?' I asked, guessing which donkey she referred to.

'Told him who else was coming, of course. As soon as he heard her ladyship was on the guest list he was up and away. I thought I'd leave the roses there and take them back to London with us. Not that I care for them all that much, but it will be my small revenge. He's fiendishly jealous, you know, that young man. Gets quite violent sometimes. It can be embarrassing. Honestly, Tessa, nobody knows what I have to put up with.'

'Not for want of being told, though. And, in the meantime, where does one wash the olive oil off one's hands?'

'Door on the left at the top of the stairs.'

It was like falling back into a half-forgotten dream, because Philip was standing with one foot on the bottom step of the narrow staircase, in the act of hauling the other one up to join it. This time, though, I did not attempt to follow him, since it could be assumed that his destination was also the door on the left at the top. Furthermore, Dolly was standing behind him, with one hand on the bannister rope, the other flattened against the opposite wall, as though forming herself into a human crash barrier. Hovering a few paces behind them and watching with a glint of amusement was Pete. None of them noticed me and considering it inadvisable to draw Clarrie into the fray, I turned in the other direction and padded silently back to the verandah, where Robin was looking predictably bored and aggrieved.

'What the hell's going on?'

'I was hoping you'd be able to tell me.'

'All I know is that after you left there was a heavy silence while Pete, or whatever his name is, sat smirking at us all and then Philip started droning on about something he'd said or done when he was on tour in South Africa until, more or less in mid-sentence, he simply nodded off. Hardly surprising really; it was a most tedious story.'

'Did one of you wake him up?'

'No, that's when it turned into pure farce. Dolly said it might be dangerous to disturb him and we'd better all keep quiet, so there we all sat; but after a few minutes he woke up by himself and began behaving like a querulous child, complaining that he wanted to go to the bathroom.'

'And then what?'

'He managed to get to his feet, with a little help from Pete, who was practically killing himself by this time, and off they all shuffled. Any chance that we could just slip away?'

'We can hardly leave Clarrie to cope with Dolly fussing, in her present state. Besides, all the pubs will be shut now and I'm starving. I doubt if I could last out till we get back to Toby's refrigerator. Tell you what, though; I'll go and see if she'd mind our helping ourselves to a slice or two of something, while Philip gets sorted out.'

'And we can't just eat and run either, so that'll mean being stuck here for at least another half hour. Oh well, do whatever you like. They're your friends.'

Feeling like a buffer state getting more than its fair share of buffeting, I trudged back indoors again and was making for the kitchen, where I could hear raised voices from Pete and Clarrie, when, ahead of me, I perceived her ladyship coming downstairs again.

'How's Philip?'

'Resting, thank you. God willing, he'll be able to get up in a few minutes and I can take him out of this bedlam.'

'It's not serious, then?'

'Not as far as I know, but all this ridiculous hanging about would be too much for anyone, after the sort of week he's been through and God knows what they put in those drinks.'

I could have told her exactly what they put in those drinks, but, not wishing to add fuel to these already raging fires, I said: 'How about something to eat, while you're waiting? Robin and I have decided to go ahead.'

'You please yourselves, my dear. Personally, I've gone past it. I only came down to tell our hostess that we shall be leaving in a few minutes.'

'She and Pete are having a conference in the kitchen.'

'How typical!' her ladyship said and jangled off to break it up.

'I hope you've no objection to our helping ourselves?' I asked Clarrie, when she and Pete joined us on the verandah about ten minutes later.

'Not at all. Be my guests!'

'We are your guests,' Robin informed her. 'Although it is not always easy to remember that.'

'Have they gone?' I asked, metaphorically thrusting myself between them.

'Yes, God be praised! Actually, poor old Philip was quite keen to stay when it came to the point, wasn't he, darling? Said he'd been momentarily overcome by waves of fatigue, but it's passed off now and a little something to eat would do him good. However, her ladyship was adamant. I have a strange feeling that she loathes the sight of me.'

'Nothing strange about it,' Pete said, 'seeing how that drunken, lecherous old husband of hers was hugging and slobbering over you.'

'Oh, nonsense, darling! That doesn't mean a thing. He does it to all the girls below the age of ninety.'

'Is that true, Tessa?' Pete demanded, placing me in the cleftest of sticks, since Robin also looked keen to hear the answer.

'Oh, well,' I said feebly. 'Well, you know how actors are?'

'No, I don't know how actors are, I'm pleased to say, but I do know how Clarrie is and, of all the sickening exhibitions, this took some beating.'

'Oh, shut up, will you, darling? Anyone would think I've had enough to put up with, without you starting on me. I was only trying to be pleasant, after all.'

'In the only way you know how!'

'Kindly stop insulting me in front of my friends, if you'll be so good? And, anyway, who invited them here in the first place and whose fault was it that Philip got so stoned he practically passed out? Just answer me that!'

It was clear that they were now boiling up to a first-class row and, by tacit consent, Robin and I set our plates down on

24

the rickety little table and, as though carrying out a well-rehearsed routine, blew some kisses into the air and silently stole away. They were both in full spate by then and hardly seemed to notice.

'How thankful I am not to have been with you!' Toby said, when we had described these goings-on.

'Yes, you'd have hated every minute, and those two getting into a drunken brawl was just about the last straw. Although, to be fair, I don't believe Pete was drunk at all. He was most abstemious where his own intake was concerned, but he's so neurotically jealous that it only needs the tiniest provocation to set him off.'

'And to be fairer still,' Robin remarked, 'I wouldn't say that Clarrie keeps him short of provocation.'

'No, she doesn't. In fact, she goes out of her way to supply it. Like all the fuss she was making over those depressing roses Oliver had brought her. I daresay that was at the back of Pete's outburst. It's hard to believe that he could genuinely regard Philip as a rival.'

'It all sounds highly distasteful and, if there ever was a love affair too hot not to cool down,' Toby said, quoting some of his favourite lines, 'I should say this was it. I see trouble ahead for them if they don't pull themselves together and grow up.'

As it happened, he was right, although the trouble, when it came, was not due to circumstances which any of us could have foreseen and was far too serious to be placed in the category of just one of those things.

CHAPTER THREE

It was on Monday, the day after Clarrie's disastrous luncheon party, that the first letter arrived and, if anything could have been better calculated to lower morale still further, I would pay someone ten thousand pounds to name it.

Not that any of us, with one notable exception, was disposed to treat it seriously at first. We concluded that one of our number had become so mentally deranged by the oppressions and apprehensions that hung over us as to have imagined it might create an amusing diversion to cheer us up. Even Philip, surprisingly enough, seeing that he was the victim, seemed as ready as anyone to dismiss it as a rather tasteless joke, but naturally no-one could have expected him to destroy the letter without so much as mentioning it to his wife and it would have been asking for a miracle to imagine that it would not then get to the ears of everyone.

She was convinced that the practical joke, if such it was, had been perpetrated by someone in the company, and unhappily, there could be no doubt that she was right. For one thing, the letter had undoubtedly been delivered by hand, since it was not inside an envelope. It was waiting for him, pinned at one corner by a jar of cold cream, when he arrived at the theatre and it was virtually inconceivable that an outsider could have got past the stage door keeper and found his way unobserved into and out of one of the dressing rooms. Moreover, even in that unlikely event, the chances of picking on a moment when it was neither occupied nor locked up must have been in the vicinity of a thousand to one.

And, in addition to this, there was yet another feature which proved it to have been an inside job, in that it contained a direct bearing on the play, and the part of the grandfather in particular, which no-one who had not read it could have known about. One of several sub-plots actually centred on an anonymous letter writer and it was the old man himself who, by a combination of sagacity and perception, was able eventually to unmask the culprit, to the great surprise of all the other characters and ultimately, we hoped, to the audience as well.

The real life message, however, was much blunter and more succinct than any of those used by the fictitious character, consisting of the single statement: *Let us eat and drink for tomorrow you die.* It must have taken time and patience to compose, though, because each word had been clipped from a newspaper headline and pasted on to a square of brown wrapping paper.

There was also a difference of opinion between her ladyship and the rest of us as to what should be done about it. Predictably enough, she was clamouring for the police to be informed without delay and there was even a hint or two that she imagined Philip's knighthood would entitle him to special protection. Fortunately, however, he was under no such illusion himself and, to our relief, was not only astute enough to be aware of the adverse publicity which would follow from police involvement, but for once had the courage to take the opposite view from Dolly's and to stick to it. He insisted that nothing should be done until Oliver had been told and the onus put on him to decide what action, if any, should be taken.

'And you know what will come of that, I suppose?' was Clarrie's rhetorical question when the unofficial conference had broken up. 'His Godliness will hand the whole business over to Redhead, who won't have the first idea how to cope.'

'Which will be the ideal solution,' I told her, 'because, between us, we can surely spike Dolly's guns and get it through to Benjie that it was just some puerile joke and nothing whatever to worry about. That'll let him off the hook and, with any luck, we'll hear no more about it.'

This turned out to be an accurate prognosis, except for its conclusion which, unhappily, was several miles wide of the mark. Benjie reacted just as we had hoped he would, but it was far from being the end of it because, when Philip returned to his room after the lunch break, the second letter was already awaiting him, propped up against a mirror. The text this time was: *The last enemy that shall be destroyed is death*, and the same device had been used of words clipped from newspaper headlines and pasted on to brown paper.

Luckily, this turned out to be one of the rare occasions when Oliver was in front throughout the afternoon session and he was still there, conferring with the director, when it ended. After a brief discussion I was delegated to convey the news to him, and I went through the pass door, up to the tenth row of the stalls and asked if he could kindly spare me a few minutes to discuss some urgent business.

He said he would be only too delighted, if I could bear to wait for just a few minutes, so I went down to the fifth row, where he joined me a quarter of an hour later, full of apologies.

Courtesy was not Oliver's only grace. He was also good-natured, cultivated and generous, always immaculately, though soberly, dressed, somewhat in the style of an exceptionally well-turned-out civil servant. In other words, as far removed as could be imagined from the popular image of a theatrical impresario and not bearing much resemblance to the reality either.

Clarrie's name for him was "His Godliness", which was apt, in a way, because he did adopt a rather sanctimonious attitude when unsure of himself, although her allusion lay in the adjacency of this attribute to cleanliness, which was Oliver's most noticeable one.

In the initial stages we had considered ourselves fortunate to have such a civilised captain at the helm, but lately some

28

doubts had crept in to erode our enthusiasm. It had made a pleasant change to have the orders from the bridge relayed in such considerate terms, less satisfactory when the orders were either indecisive or not forthcoming at all. The feeling had been growing that a coarser spirit might have been more effective in steering us through these troubled waters.

His reaction to the latest news was fairly typical: 'Oh, not another? Poor old Philip! How absolutely abominable! Ought I to go and commiserate?'

'No, I think he's gone home now.'

'So not too upset about it?' Oliver asked, looking relieved.

'Not as badly as most people would have been, perhaps. In fact, he's keeping amazingly cool, all things considered, but I'm afraid the same can't be said of Dolly. She's the one who's kicking up the row. She wishes to know what you intend to do about it.'

'And I only wish I could tell her, my dearest. The problem is that I hardly see what anyone can do about it, short of handing it over to the police and I gather from Benjie that, on the whole, you wouldn't be in favour of that?'

'No, we're not. It's accepted that they can be very discreet, but even so they'd have to question everyone in the company, including, with no exceptions, all the technicians and stage hands. There'd simply be no other way of handling it and that certainly wouldn't create a very harmonious atmosphere during the run-up to the first night.'

'Most likely down tools to a man.'

'And, apart from that, Oliver, the news would inevitably get leaked to the press, wouldn't you say? I know that, in theory, all publicity is good publicity, but I have a nasty feeling that this story could so easily rebound on us.'

'You're absolutely right, of course, and so what are we left with? Absolute stalemate, as far as I can see.'

'There might be one alternative.'

'Might there, really? Do tell me!'

29

'A sort of compromise, in a way. That's to say, not bringing the police in officially, but . . .'

I tailed off here because Oliver was regarding me with an
expression I could not interpret. There seemed to be amusement in it, but wariness too.

'What's funny?' I asked him.

'Forgive me, Tessa, but I have heard something about your
activities in the crime world. I imagine everyone has, after
that sensation in Dearehaven last summer. I was just wondering whether you proposed to take this on yourself, a sort of
one-woman investigation?'

'No, certainly not. I can just imagine how popular that
would make me, can't you? Besides, I trust it hasn't escaped
your notice that I happen to be working quite hard already,
just at present?'

'Yes, indeed, and please forgive me! If only they were all
like you . . . Well, tell me then, what kind of compromise had
you in mind?'

'I persuaded Philip not to destroy the letters, which was
what he wanted to do, but to let me borrow them for a few
hours, so that I could show them to Robin.'

'Robin?'

'The man I'm married to. He's a real detective, as you may
already know, not an amateur like me, but a C.I.D. Inspector
with heaps of experience. It's true that I was in a special
position to dig out one or two facts in the Dearehaven case,
which helped to sort out the goats from the sheep, but I
shouldn't have got anywhere without Robin's expertise to
back it up. So just now, after the Mickletons had gone, I put it
to one or two of the others that I should show him the letters
and see if there was anything about them that struck him as in
any way familiar. They agreed that it would be a terrific idea,
but I thought I ought to clear it with you first, in case you had
any objection.'

The concluding words had been thrown in for form's sake

because the offer had been received with so much enthusiasm from everyone else that I had expected as much, if not more of the same from Oliver. It was something of a jolt to find it greeted with a tight-lipped silence. He had removed his spectacles too, and was polishing them on one of the pristine, monogrammed handkerchiefs, always a sign of turmoils of indecision raging beneath the urbane exterior.

'Well?' I asked, when he still did not speak.

'I don't know, Tessa. I do realise that you're only trying to be constructive and I certainly have no wish to offend you, but quite frankly I do jib at the idea of the word getting around outside.'

'But it will be entirely unofficial and confidential. Surely I made that clear?'

'It's not that which worries me.'

'What, then?'

'Simply that I feel very strongly that, by taking any action of the kind you suggest, we shall simply be playing into the hands of this lunatic, reacting just as he'd hoped we would. If we accept, as I suppose we are bound to, that he will be just as well informed as everyone else about what you propose to do, that will be one up to him, won't it? He'll have got us on the hop. Whereas, if all we innocent bystanders, individually and collectively, can manage to create the impression that we regard the letters as some petty, childish joke, nothing for adult people to get upset about, then he will soon realise that there is no point in going on with the game. I honestly believe that this is the best way to deal with the situation and, if you think about it, I'm sure you'll come round to my point of view.'

As it happened, I had thought about it already and I was nowhere near coming round to his point of view. In fact, in my opinion, he had gravely underrated the risks in the course he was now advocating and the damage to morale which would ensue if it did not pay off. I had small hope of Robin being able to solve the mystery, or point to the identity of Anon simply by looking at the letters, but I was still convinced that everyone concerned would feel more comfortable if action of some kind could be seen to be taken, whether it brought results or not.

However, like most vacillators, Oliver could be stubborn too on occasion and nothing would budge him from his position, so in the end we reached a rather uneasy compromise. If, during the forthcoming twenty-four hours, no further letters arrived, we should all do our utmost to put the matter out of our minds and carry on as though nothing had happened. On the other hand, if the joke, or whatever it was, were to be prolonged into the following day, I had his full permission to enlist Robin's help.

I cannot be sure what I should have done if he had then asked me to hand over the letters to him for safe keeping, but, luckily, he did not. It was a rather curious oversight too, in my opinion, for I would certainly have expected such a clever man as he was to guess that I had not the smallest intention of sticking to my side of the bargain.

CHAPTER FOUR

I

To my annoyance, the following day began with a victory for Oliver, vindicating his policy of 'when in doubt what to do, do nothing', because there was no letter waiting for Philip and none arrived during the whole of that rehearsal session.

Naturally, I was not disposed to complain about this; the annoyance came from the thought of him preening himself on the success of his tactics, whereas I, who had the power to disabuse him, was prevented by my own duplicity from using it.

As he had pointed out, there could be no doubt that Anon had been as well informed as anyone about my plan to consult Robin and I had credited him with rather more astuteness than Oliver in foreseeing that I should go ahead with it, with or without the management's blessing, particularly since I had not bothered to mention that such blessing had been withheld. It was my firm opinion that it was not so much the pretence of indifference to his activities which had induced him to give them up as the discovery that, against all the odds, an official from Scotland Yard had been informed of them.

If so, it would no doubt have come as a relief to him to know that Robin's verdict had been practically worthless, but I did not see fit to mention this either, least of all to Clarrie. Indeed, she would have been the last person I would have confided in, since the single odd feature common to both letters which Robin had drawn my attention to pointed to her as the possible author.

'Whatever gave you that idea?' I asked him.

'Hadn't you noticed the Biblical touch?'

'Yes, subconsciously, I suppose I had, but isn't that the kind of language one automatically associates with anonymous letter writers? I had always assumed that it was a way of implying that the message did not come from them, personally, that they were merely acting as instruments of the Almighty?'

'Yes, very likely, in some cases, but we know that this was not the work of some Bible-thumping crackpot. They were sent, you maintain, by someone well known to you all, who is outwardly just as sane as you are, and of all the possible candidates isn't Clarrie the one who stands out as being on familiar terms with the Bible?'

'Well, that's true, of course, although nowadays she doesn't quote from it so often as she used to. I don't know whether that's because it started out as an affectation, some childish desire to shock, which she has now grown out of, or whether it was so much a part of the language she grew up with that for a long time it came naturally to her.'

'Whatever the reason, it still might not occur to her what a give-away it was.'

'Well, yes, that may be so, but we seem to be arguing over technicalities and nothing can alter the fact that it's not in character for Clarrie to do a thing like this. Whatever else, she's not sly and, besides, what possible motive, real of imaginary, could she have?'

'I'm afraid I can't help you there, that would be for you to find out. You asked me if I could dig out any clue, however fragile, to Anon's identity and I have to admit that, so far, this is the only one to strike me. Of course, if I were to borrow the letters and have them put through the routine mill, it might produce something to start you off, but I doubt it very much. I imagine it's been handled and mangled and puffed over by at least half a dozen people?'

'At least. And by none more thoroughly than Clarrie, I might add.'

'Which could have had a purpose and could have been straightforward, innocent curiosity. The trouble you have here, as so often in the past, is that you're up against a mob of people for whom life consists largely of pretending to be what they are not and who, over the years, have become rather practised in it.'

'So, if another letter does turn up, what do you advise us to do? And please don't say we should all play along with Oliver and pretend it isn't happening. For one thing, her ladyship is not in a mood to co-operate and I wouldn't put it past her to take matters into her own hands and call the police in off her own bat. That could have catastrophic results and, even without it, there'd be all sorts of worries and tensions to keep us on edge, which is hardly what we need, with the dress rehearsal only twenty-four hours away.'

'Yes, it's a depressing outlook, I agree; although it does sound from what you tell me that the victim himself remains comparatively unmoved?'

'That's true. It scarcely seems to have got through to Philip, but that may be just one more sign of encroaching senility, which doesn't do much to cheer one up.'

'You wouldn't accept the idea that, unlike the rest of you, he has a shrewd idea of who did send the letters and therefore feels confident that he has nothing to fear?'

'Oh no, that doesn't sound at all likely. If it were so, why wouldn't he have tipped off her ladyship and stopped her ranting around and screaming for vengeance?'

'Yes, that's logical, I suppose.'

'So what do you advise?'

'As far as I can see, you haven't much choice. You had better take a leaf from Clarrie's book and put your faith in God to strike down your enemy. Or at least stay his hand.'

I cannot pretend that mine was of the strength to move mountains, so presumably other forces must have been at work in restraining him and granting us a reprieve, for the worst that happened on Tuesday morning was getting seized on by Dolly, who was present when I gave Philip back the letters and commanded me to give her a detailed account of Robin's reaction to them. I managed to fob her off by saying that, from his experience of these matters, he did not consider that we should take this one too seriously. He had seen a great many communications of this type and had developed a sixth sense, which rarely let him down, enabling him to distinguish on sight between those which posed a genuine threat and the vast majority which came from some harmless lunatic with a misplaced sense of humour. Most of this was twaddle, needless to say, but, although obviously far from satisfied, she consented to abide by this verdict, pending further developments.

II

The next airing of the subject, which was naturally at the back of all our minds, and not so far back either, took place a few hours later between Clarrie and myself and an actor named Anthony Blewiston, who had a walk-on and also understudied Philip.

Clarrie, all agog for Robin's report, had asked me to meet her for lunch in a pub round the corner, about five minutes' walk from the theatre. It was an overheated, smoke-laden little place, with a regular and predominantly male clientele, most of whom looked as though they had met there to clinch the final details on some shady racecourse deal, but at least there were no fruit machines or space games to distract them from their business and, as they all talked in undertones, the decibel level was acceptable.

I was only a little late for our appointment and was therefore slightly annoyed to find that Anthony, who had wandered in on his own a few minutes ahead of me, had already been invited to join us. However, I resigned myself to the fact that it was probably asking too much to expect Clarrie to be left sitting on her own in a public place for more than five seconds at a stretch. On the whole, I could consider myself fortunate that on this occasion she had at least pulled a well-mannered and presentable fish into her net.

He was a tall, good-looking, soldierly sort of man, aged about fifty, which of course was far too young for the part of the grandfather and, since it was becoming increasingly likely that sooner or later he would be called upon to play it, this had created an additional obstacle in our battle to survive.

It was not only his comparative youth, either, which was against him, for in fact he neither was, nor appeared ever to have made the smallest effort to be, more than a third-rate actor. Presumably, it was his looks and charm which had encouraged him, or made other people encourage him to take up acting as a profession, but they had not been enough and he, so easy-going and confident in real life, unfailingly turned into a block of boring wood the instant he set foot on a stage. Perhaps, if he had worked on it, he might have improved, but he was unable to take himself seriously enough to rise above the mediocre and he was also totally lacking in ambition. His chief delights in life were hunting, polo and riding in point-to-points, any activity, in fact, which required the active participation of horses, and in spending as much time as was consistent with earning a living on the modest estate he had inherited in Sussex. Presumably, the reason why he obtained enough work throughout the year to indulge himself in this way was that even in middle age his appearance, for an actor, was unusual enough to keep him in demand for character parts with a military or aristocratic background and, perhaps equally important, because he was so modest and amiable as to make him a pleasure to work with.

Inevitably, he was known to some people as Moody Blues, which was easily the most inappropriate nickname ever invented, but this did not appear to worry him in the least and, in my experience, the only thing that ruffled his good nature was when someone addressed him as Tony.

Naturally, he was in no danger of being affronted in this way by Clarrie, who stuck to her self-imposed rule and called him by whatever endearment sprang to mind.

'Well, come on, Tessa! Don't just sit there, say something!' she commanded me when Anthony had ordered the moussaka three times, with salad on the side.

'Like what?'

'What Robin thought about the letters, fool! Was he inspired?'

'Not at all. Inspiration doesn't play much part in his approach to these matters. And, in any case his comments, such as they were, are now out of date, since he is no longer in full possession of the facts.'

'Can you make head or tail of this jargon, dearest?' Clarrie asked.

'Neither h nor t. Do stop playing the bobby on the beat, Tessa!'

'Very well, here it is in plain language. When I talked to Robin yesterday evening and showed him the letters there were two of them and now there are three. How's that for clarity?'

'Three?' she repeated. 'Since when?'

'Since about twenty minutes ago. It was why I was late getting here. Number three was waiting on his shelf, exactly like the others. He brought it along to my room and asked me what he should do about it.'

'Why you?'

'Why not her? Anthony asked. 'He thinks she's the Delphic Oracle and Hercule Poirot rolled into one, everyone knows that. It's a hangover from dandling her on his knee when she was two years old.'

'Dolly had already left, you see,' I explained. 'Gone to a fitting for her ball gown for the first night, I gather. So that clinches it, doesn't it?'

'Clinches what?'

'The fact that this vendetta is the work of someone very close to us. We can't any longer pretend it's some demented stage hand with a long-standing grievance against Philip, who seduced his daughter in nineteen hundred and two. No one of that sort could have known that her ladyship had an appointment with her dressmaker at twelve o'clock and therefore the coast would be clear.'

'Did he show you the letter?'

'Oh yes, he was waving it under my nose. He was in quite a tizzy about this one. Not scared, as far as I could make out, but highly incensed about the invasion of his privacy. He is getting absolutely sick of it, if we want to know.'

'And was it just like the others? What did it say?'

I was glad it was Clarrie who had put this question because it allowed me to study her expression as I replied: 'The format was the same. Newspaper clippings pasted on brown paper, as before, but there was a slight change in the prose style. The message this time was: *Beware that sleep of death*.'

They had both laid down their forks, the better to pay attention and Anthony said: 'You mean more specific than the others?'

I was still watching Clarrie, as I answered: 'No, that wasn't what I meant, although it's true, of course; but the big difference was that this one had a Shakespearian flavour about it, whereas the other two were based on phrases from the Bible.'

'Yes, they were, weren't they?' she agreed, sounding quite cheerful about it. 'I noticed that too. Could you be an angel, darling, and ask them to bring me a glass of their impudent little red? It's probably fatal, but this tarted up shepherd's pie really does need a little help. You know, Tessa, when the second letter arrived I began to wonder whether someone was putting those Bible bits in to make it look as though it were me.'

'Robin had much the same idea.'

'Did he now? He's sharp, that boy of yours, isn't he? Oh, thank you, darling! And one for Tessa and yourself as well! That makes me feel much less conspicuous and self-indulgent. I suppose he didn't have any bright ideas about who might be playing such a dirty trick?'

I shook my head, not wishing to interrupt the flow.

'Because, I mean, when you get right down to it, why would I want to mount a campaign to scare poor old Philip into a jelly? I do have my faults, as you may or may not know, but no one could call me spiteful. And anyway stirring up trouble has never been my game. He that sows the wind shall reap the whirlwind, which is the last thing I want to reap.'

'If you ask me,' Anthony said, 'whoever's responsible for this business must not only be spiteful, but also half-witted if it hasn't sunk in yet that their effect on Philip has been practically negligible. So far, there hasn't been the whisper of a whirlwind from that quarter.'

'You can bet your life there will be though, darling, when her ladyship gets to hear about the latest outrage. She only agreed to hold her horses on condition that no more letters turned up. Think he means to tell her about this new one, Tessa?'

'With any luck, he may not. I suggested that it would only distress her and that there was nothing to be gained by it.'

'Did he agree?'

'Seemed to. That's what really staggers me about Philip's whole attitude.'

'Taking it so coolly, you mean?'

'Not only that, but he doesn't seem to recognise any connection between cause and effect, or the possibility of a bad thing leading to a worse. So far as he's concerned, it seems to resolve itself into the simple question of whether or not to inform the police. Apparently, it hasn't occurred to him that there could be any real threat behind it, or that his life might actually be in danger.'

'And you consider that to be over-optimistic?'

'I honestly don't know, Anthony. It was one of the things I specially wanted to ask Robin about. Whether threats of this kind usually mean business, or whether they're more likely to be an end in themselves.'

'And what was his answer?'

'More or less on the lines of your guess is as good as mine. He said it was mostly the second, but there were enough instances of letters being followed up by murder, or attempted murder, never to rule it out. And I may say that, if I were Philip, the odds wouldn't be long enough for me.'

'So, after all, you're on her ladyship's side?' Clarrie said, 'You think he should be given some kind of protection and blow all the rumpus when the news got around?'

'Not necessarily, because I don't see how that kind of protection could be effective. Since it's now accepted that Anon is one of us, then obviously the one place where he should be safe, which is inside the theatre, becomes the one where he is most vulnerable.'

'Quite so,' Anthony agreed, 'and, furthermore, if I were Anon, which I sometimes think I may be when I look at Philip, and were planning to put words into deeds, I know the precise moment I should choose for it. The fact that Anon appears to have the same idea is not very heartening for me.'

'I suppose you mean that scene in the play where Philip falls asleep and has to be shaken into life? I agree that it ties in very neatly with Anon's latest message, but I shouldn't let that worry you. I'm sure you're not the only one who has realised that, if someone were really out to finish off Philip and the play all in one swipe, that would be the most effective way to do it.'

'I may not be the only one who's thought of it, but it still leaves me in a rather special position.'

41

'How do you work that out?'

'Well, you see, I am not only the one who pours out his cold tea in the scene which comes before that one, but what more satisfactory suspect than the poor old understudy?'

'No, that won't do at all, Anthony, not in your case. Everyone knows you'd be bored out of your mind if you had to wade through a part like that eight times a week. And even if you had been fooling us all these years and nursing secret ambitions to become the big star, you know very well that wouldn't be the way to go about it. The curtain would come down half way through the first act, never to rise again. So you not only wouldn't step into dead man's shoes, you'd be out of a job and might even be forced into putting one of those hunters up for sale.'

'Besides, how about me?' Clarrie asked in a complaining voice, evidently resentful at being left out of this game, 'You've both forgotten me, I suppose?'

'No, dear, certainly not. How could one ever do that? Do you need more wine?'

'No, but perhaps I'm a schizo too, unbeknownst to everyone, including myself. Not only retreating back into my guilt-laden childhood and chucking Biblical quotes around, but just ask yourselves this? Who is it in the play who is finally exposed as the one who's been sending anonymous letters and who does the exposing?'

'Yes,' Anthony agreed thoughtfully, 'that's a damned interesting theory and I can see the force of it. You have become so divorced from reality that you have ceased to distinguish between your theatrical identity and the real one? It would appear to be taking the Method rather to extremes, but what would that matter to someone as mixed up as you now tell us you are?'

'And just think how well placed we shall be,' I reminded them, 'if we do get a murder! Here we are with no less than two prime suspects making out two irrefutable cases against themselves before it has even been committed. That must be quite rare in the annals of crime.'

'Have we overdone it, darling?' Clarrie asked anxiously. 'She wouldn't be beginning to take us seriously, would she? I shall deny every word, you know, Tessa, if someone does have a go.'

'So shall I,' Anthony said. 'On my word of honour, as an actor and a gentleman!'

'Oh, don't worry,' I assured them. 'No-one understands better than I do that this flippancy is simply a way of relieving the nervous tension, because at heart you're both dead scared, like everyone else, with the exception of Philip, that something terrible is waiting for us round the next corner. Besides, if it's any comfort to you . . .'

'Oh yes, almost anything could be counted as a comfort just now. What have you got for us?'

'If it should come to the worst, I already have a much more promising culprit lined up than either of you two.'

Fortunately, perhaps, since this grandiose claim was based simply on a casual remark of Toby's, neither of them seemed disposed to take it any more seriously than what had gone before, nor were they at all eager for me to enlarge on it and a few minutes afterwards we all went our separate ways, to reassemble at six o'clock for the dress rehearsal.

III

'How did it go?' Robin asked me, when I arrived home soon after midnight, then responding to my grimace went on without a pause, 'Oh, cheer up! Isn't there a saying about bad dress rehearsals being the prelude to crackling first nights?'

'If it's true, this first night is going to crackle so merrily that the circle and gallery will burst into flames.'

'Well, it won't help to sit here doing the post mortem for a couple of hours. Why not drag yourself upstairs and I'll bring you a lovely hot drink in bed?'

'And at least you were spared the ultimate disaster, I take it?' he said, putting the mug down on my bedside table about ten minutes later, 'or did you forget to mention that there'd been a sudden death to add to your problems?'

'No, we all came out of it alive, as it happens; which ought to have been a huge relief, of course, only in a funny way it wasn't. What did you put in this drink by the way? It's doing me good.'

'Just hot milk, nutmeg and a dash, maybe two. In what sort of funny way wasn't it a huge relief?'

'Well, you see, it was as though we'd been holding our breath and bracing ourselves for the moment when Philip's supposed to fall asleep and for his literally never waking up again. I imagine several others, apart from Clarrie and Anthony and myself, had picked up the idea that, if anything were going to happen, this would be the moment.'

'But nothing did happen?'

'Nothing at all. In fact, for once it went like clockwork. Peter crossed on cue and gave Philip a gentle nudge, you could almost read his mind, poor Peter, whereupon Philip shot up, opened his eyes and went straight into his next line. Getting it right too, which you could say was epoch-making in its way. I'm ashamed to say I was the one who fluffed.'

'Quite understandable. It was the shock that did it.'

'You're so right! The kind of shock which would come from falling from the tenth storey and finding yourself able to get up and walk back upstairs again. It was unforgivable, just the same, because that kind of lapse is contagious and from then on things began falling apart all over the place. It's hard to describe, but it's as though it had been the tension which had held us together and, once that was gone, all the stuffing seemed to ooze away.'

'Yes, I can understand that and also why you all regarded that particular scene as the crucial one, but what does puzzle me is why you'd got it so firmly fixed in your minds that tonight would be the night?'

'Oh, didn't I tell you? No, of course I didn't, how stupid! There'd been another letter, you see. It was there when he came in this evening. He and Dolly were the last to arrive. There'd been some mix-up, apparently, about whether she would collect him from the flat, or whether they'd meet at the theatre and, as a result, she arived first and was the first to see it, so there was no concealing it from her this time. Anyway, it means that anyone at all could have planted it there and we're as far away as ever from finding out who actually did.'

'And that brings me to something else I don't understand. Aren't the rooms locked when they're not in use?'

'In theory, yes, but not always in practice. Added to which, it wouldn't have been much trouble to have got hold of a spare key and had a duplicate made. There's a locksmith round the corner who does them while you wait.'

'And there's his dresser, of course. He'd have a key. I suppose he must rank fairly high on the list of suspects?'

'Not really, Robin. For one thing, he's never worked for Philip before, and also he hasn't been around until quite recently, certainly not during the period when the first letter arrived.'

'I see! And what form did the latest one take? Bible or Shakespeare?'

'Neither. It just said: *Curtains tonight*. Very down to earth and straight to the point.'

'But, since it didn't come to the point, doesn't it sound after all as though this is just some elaborate joke?'

'If so, it's not giving rise to much mirth, I can assure you. I think what's depressing us now is knowing that we've got to go through the whole dreary business again tomorrow night and perhaps the one after that, and on and on, never able to relax and put it out of our minds. I shouldn't be surprised if one of us were to murder him, just to put an end to the suspense.'

'Well, try not to worry any more tonight. And don't forget that if something should happen tomorrow, I'll be out in front, watching every move and gesture with hawk-eyed attention.'

'Then I'll get the stage manager to come on and say: "Ladies and Gentlemen, is there a policeman in the house?" and you can tear round and sort it out within ten minutes of the crime being committed. So at least your career won't suffer, even if mine goes into decline.'

'On which consoling note,' Robin said, 'I suggest you try and get some sleep now and I shall do likewise. It begins to look as though we may both have a heavy day ahead of us.'

CHAPTER FIVE

Always willing and usually able to oblige, I switched off the light and obediently fell asleep for approximately ten hours. It worked wonders too, because by midday on a sunny May morning the world had polished up its image and I had become a born-again optimist.

There was no rational way to account for it, but I was not altogether surprised when I arrived at my place of work to find that other people had been similarly affected. It does not need to be said that, like me, most of them had become rigid with terror, with damp palms, dry mouths and a slight, though perpetual sense of nausea, but first-night nerves are a familiar horror, something to be accepted and lived through by means of well-tried tricks and disciplines. This time, I suspected, I was not alone in welcoming them as old friends, since, by turning up so punctually, they had somehow contrived to push the unfamiliar fears, if not out out of existence, at least into perspective. It even crossed my mind that Philip's extraordinary composure and apparent indifference to the threats which had been made against him was not just another sign that he was losing his grip, but that on the contrary, it proved him to possess more common sense than the rest of us put together.

Inevitably, the see-saw began to tilt the other way as soon as the curtain was up, for that was the signal for the other queasiness to start draining away and, to some extent, to be replaced by the nebulous fears of the past few days. Even so, they did not return with the same force as during the dress rehearsal, because long before we got to the dreaded scene where the young man made his impassioned appeal to the

47

sleeping grandfather we had sensed that things were going well, with laughs coming in unexpected places, and nothing can quite subdue the exhilaration which bubbles up at times like these. Furthermore, although I could not see him, I could judge to within inches where Robin was sitting and this also contributed to my soaring confidence. It was just as well that I had a lot of smiling and crowing to do when I made my entrance, pointed out to my brother-in-law that he had been wasting his oratory and then stood by, watching him wake up his grandfather. Nothing had ever gone more smoothly and Philip, who had got a round of applause when he first came on, timed it to perfection.

All good things must come to an end, however and the first intimation that the pendulum was beginning to swing the other way came about twenty minutes after the final curtain, when Clarrie came bursting into my dressing room. Two or three gushing friends had come and gone, but Robin was still there and our cosy, self-congratulatory session came to an abrupt end when we saw that she was wearing a kimono, still had her stage make-up on and that it did nothing at all to mask her fury and mortification.

'Anything wrong?' I asked, pouring her a drink from the bottle which Robin had thoughtfully had sent round to the theatre a few hours earlier.

'Just that I've been stood up, humiliated and abandoned, if you call that wrong.'

'By Pete?'

'Who else?'

'You mean he's reclining in someone else's dressing room tonight?'

'Well, he certainly isn't reclining in mine. Not much fun, is it? I'm sick to death of it, as Philip would say. Here am I, all strung up like a guitar, waiting to be smothered by praise and made a great fuss of and what happens? Damn bloody all! Not so much as a kind word and a pat on the back.'

'Was he in front?'

'No, he and her ladyship are saving themselves for the first night.'

'Oh well, don't worry, in that case. He'll be here in a minute. Probably got caught up in a traffic jam.'

'If so, he was travelling in the wrong direction. You don't know how lucky you are to have Old Reliable here,' Clarrie said, giving Robin a seductive smile, either to compensate for having forgotten his name, or because the wine was getting her back to normal.

'What did you mean by "travelling in the wrong direction"?' he asked her.

'Well, you see, darling, if he's in a traffic jam, he must be driving away from the theatre and not coming towards it. It follows as the night the day.'

'Meaning that he was here earlier?'

'Oh, he's a bright one, isn't he, Tessa? Yes, that is what I mean. He was here in the interval and he was still here when I did my change in the second half. Now he's gone. Fine thing, isn't it?'

Before we could tell her whether it was or not, there was a knock on the door and when I shouted 'Come In!' it opened just wide enough for Pete to put his head round.

'Sorry to intrude, Tessa, but you wouldn't happen to know where . . . Oh, there you are, Clarrie! I was afraid I'd lost you.'

'Another five minutes and you would have.'

'Terribly sorry, darling. The silly thing is that I got stuck in a traffic jam.'

'Oh, yes? And have you anything else to tell me before we part for ever?'

'No, really, love, it's the truth. Oh, hello, Robin,' he said, coming all the way in now, 'do excuse all this. The fact is, Clarrie dearest, I bought you a little pressie this afternoon. I meant to give it to you after the show, but then I realised that, like a fool, I'd gone and left it on my desk at the shop. So I thought I'd just have time to retrieve it and be back before you came off. I would have too, if Shaftsbury Avenue hadn't been blocked from end to end. There was some charity show coming out, with one of the Royals there and I got held up for over twenty minutes.'

'What sort of present? Ice cream?'

'No, no, something a bit more solid.'

'I just wondered why it wouldn't have kept until tomorrow?'

'Oh well, you see, darling, I'd left it in full view on my desk and I was afraid it might have gone away by tomorrow. Some of those cleaning ladies we get now are not all they might be.'

I could tell that Robin was reaching the limits of boredom and irritability at having to sit through yet another of their wrangles, so I said in my Nanny voice: 'Never mind! All's well that something or other, so why not buzz along and open your present, Clarrie, and see if it's worth the price of your forgiveness?'

'And let you two get off home, is what you mean? Okay, love, see you in the morning, and make sure you don't get held up in the traffic. Thanks for the drink. Come on, you bastard, let's leave them in peace.'

It was certainly an evening for people getting mislaid, because when Pete opened the door and stood aside to let Clarrie go first, she found her way was blocked by Philip on the other side of it. He was red in the face, with mouth hanging open and he said in a bemused voice: 'Oh, Clarrie . . . is this your room? Sorry, darling, made a mistake. It was Tessa I wanted.'

Not daring to look at Robin, I called out: 'Come in, Philip! Is anything the matter?'

'No, I'm a bit bothered, that's all. I wondered if you'd seen Dolly?'

'Not this evening. Why?'

'I can't think where she's got to.'

'What time did she leave?' I asked, my mind still stuck in the same groove.

'Leave the flat, you mean? How should I know? Mind if I sit down for a minute?'

'No, of course not, go ahead! How about a drink?'

'Thanks. A scotch would do, if you have any.'

'Let me see to it,' Pete offered, causing Robin to bounce up like an infuriated rubber ball.

'I think I can manage, thank you. Pete.'

Returning my attention to Philip, I said: 'What I meant was, do you know what time she left here?'

'Haven't the faintest idea what you're talking about, my dear girl,' he said, looking slightly more alert, as he held out his hand for the glass which Robin was bringing over to him. 'Far as I'm aware, she hasn't been here since she dropped me off just before six o'clock.'

'Oh, really? Why not?'

'Because that's the routine. I like to spend an hour or two on my own before a preview or first night and I've got Fred to look after me, if I need anything. Dolly understands all about that and we arranged that she'd come back here about nine-thirty, to drive me home. Naturally, I'm worried and put out when she doesn't turn up. Who wouldn't be?'

'Probably got stuck in a traffic jam,' Robin remarked gloomily.

'Yes, as a matter of fact, that is the most likely explanation Philip. Pete has just been telling us that it's fairly chaotic out there tonight. I daresay she's arrived by now and is waiting for you, in your room, even as we speak.'

'No, she's not, or I'd have heard about it. Fred knows where to find me.'

'Have you tried telephoning?'

'Naturally! I'm not an imbecile. There was no reply.'

'There you are, then! Sitting in traffic, for sure.'

51

'Most unlike her, if she is. She always leaves plenty of extra time for that sort of emergency. Oh well, I suppose I'll have to give it a few more minutes and then start walking. Not much chance of finding a taxi, if it's as bad as you say. Thanks for the drink. It went rather well tonight, wouldn't you say?'

'No need to walk,' I said, as he started to clamber to his feet. 'We can give you a lift. We were on the point of leaving anyway and Robin's car is only two minutes away, so he can bring it round to the front for us. Meet you downstairs in five minutes, but there's no rush. He's always so lucky in that way,' I explained, 'doesn't seem to have as much trouble as the rest of us with parking restrictions.'

The Mickleton's flat was on the second floor of an Edwardian building in a seedy little street between Russell Square and the Tottenham Court Road. It was only a short distance from the theatre, but in the diametrically opposite direction from our own dear home and Philip's allowance of five minutes had been stretched to nearer fifteen by the time we set off. However, the journey was the least of our troubles because it was only on arrival that he discovered that he had left home without his keys.

'Can't understand it,' he kept muttering, while patting himself and going through each pocket twice over. 'Must be here somewhere.'

They were not, though, and I suggested he should try ringing his own bell on the row of buttons by the outer door, on the off-chance that Dolly was at home and not sitting in a traffic jam; but no disembodied voice came through the loud speaker to enquire who was without. It was deadlock, in the truest sense, until Robin noticed that there was also a bell to summon the caretaker and, after keeping his thumb pressed down on it for a full minute, we were rewarded by signs of activity in the basement. Then a window was raised and a man's voice shouted: 'What's going on up there? Do you know what time it is?'

'Eleven twenty-five,' Robin replied, 'and please come along up, will you? We need your keys.'

Perhaps this caretaker was an old lag and recognised the voice of authority, because his manner changed with the speed of lightning and a few minutes later we were able to hand Philip over to him and to be on our way home at last.

I was thankful for this at the time, but my relief then was nothing to what I was to feel when I discovered how lightly, in fact, we had been let off. Had we gone the whole way and seen Philip into his flat, we must have been confronted, as he was, by the sight of his wife sagging full length on the sitting room sofa, where she had been since approximately half past six in the evening, when she was strangled to death with one of her own silk scarves.

CHAPTER SIX

I

From the moment of this painful discovery *Elders and Betters* no longer had any real chance of survival, although for a time we forced ourselves to go believing that something could still be salvaged from the wreck and not all the signs were discouraging. A rehearsal was called for ten o'clock on Thursday morning, which Anthony managed to stumble through without disgracing himself and, after an interval of exactly twelve minutes, the curtain went up again on the afternoon preview, which also passed off without major disaster. Best of all, by six o'clock the advance bookings had taken a heady upward turn. If not to be described as a stampede, it was a situation which any management, let alone a tyro, would have regarded as satisfactory.

No doubt aware of this, and perhaps also aware that the greater part of these bookings had come from ghoulish readers of the obituary columns, Philip bravely insisted on going on for the official opening, for neither he nor anyone else could doubt that the cancellations would have streamed in just as rapidly once the word got around that he had been replaced by a practically unknown actor, whose wife had not been strangled the night before.

It was misplaced courage, however, as became plain from his first entrance. He managed to struggle on through the first half, his performance deteriorating by the minute, but, back in his dressing room in the interval, he finally collapsed and had to be driven home by ambulance.

Home, by that time, had become the first-floor spare bedroom and bath at our house in Beacon Square. Robin was not ecstatic about this arrangement and I cannot pretend that it pleased me either. Normally, these apartments are kept at the permanent disposal of my cousin Toby, who in return allows us to spend frequent weekends at his house in the country, but the situation had been more or less forced on us. Philip could hardly have been expected to remain at the flat on his own and, apart from a step-daughter, married, divorced and with two sons, left over from Dolly's first marriage and living in South Africa, neither of the Mickletons appeared to have any close relatives. Of the few remaining friends and colleagues whom she had not entirely succeeded in alienating by her jealousy and possessiveness, it seemed that we were the only pair in possession of a first-floor bedroom and bath within a taxi ride of the theatre.

The decision whereby he would occupy them until such time as things got sorted out was arrived at during the early hours of Thursday morning, Philip and the caretaker, between them, having managed to rouse one of the neighbours, who had summoned the police. It was on their advice, at the conclusion of their preliminary investigations and Dolly's removal to the mortuary, that he had applied to us and, by eight o'clock that morning, had been collected by Robin and put to bed in his temporary lodgings.

I was still less pleased when his second journey there, some twelve hours later, was made by ambulance, since this was far from being my concept of getting things off to a good start in the sorting-out process, but he was most unwilling to be sent to a hospital or nursing home, literally reduced to tears by the suggestion, and the doctor assured us that, in any case, his condition was not serious enough to warrant it. His heart, pulse and blood pressure were all in good shape, considering his age and the devastating shock he had sustained and all he needed now was a few days of complete rest and quiet.

'With you waiting on him hand and foot, I shouldn't wonder,' Robin commented gloomily.

'Yes, I have a feeling that he is going to be rather a demanding patient and, unfortunately, I'll very soon no longer have
the excuse that I'm working.'

'As bad as that?'

'Well, we still have the reviews to come, of course, but
Oliver told me at the wake tonight that, if they're as bad as he
expects them to be, the notices will have to go up tonight. He
has to concentrate now on cutting his losses. Poor Oliver! I do
feel sorry for him.'

'Well, our own papers arrived while you were taking the
invalid his breakfast in bed, so we had better draw a deep
breath and start on them. I think I've just time before I go and
get on with some bread-winning for three.'

It proved not to be such an icy plunge, after all; more of a
tepid splash, which continued to douse us throughout the day
and early evening, for none of the critics had set out to annihi-
late the play. There were mutterings about its being under-
rehearsed and partially inaudible, as well as the usual com-
plaints about the director not having made up his mind
whether he was producing a farce or a comedy or neither, but
on the other hand there were several kind words for the
author and in almost every review one or two members of the
cast had been picked out for honourable mention. Even
Anthony had been awarded one of these nosegays, for being
such a gallant trouper. In view of his performance, I concluded that he and the reviewer had been at Harrow together.

However, as everyone knows, this kind of damning with
faint praise can be more damaging than outright abuse and so
it proved for us. When we arrived at the theatre for the second
performance it was to play to less than half capacity. This was
saddening, but by no means unexpected. The real shock had
come earlier than that, during the late afternoon, when I learnt

that Pete had then spent four hours in what is technically known as helping the police with their enquiries.

II

I had come downstairs, after taking Philip a cup of tea, when Clarrie rang up and, never being one to bite back the tears, went straight into the high tragedy act, though with so much inartistic caterwaul thrown in that it was difficult to make out what she was saying.

'Just try and calm down, will you, Clarrie, and tell me what's happened?'

'I just have told you, for God's sake! Are you deaf or something? Pete's been arrested.'

'What for?'

'How would I know what for? Murdering her ladyship, I suppose. They didn't say.'

Don't be silly, they must have said. They don't just go around arresting people without telling them what they're being charged with.'

'All I know is that they said they wanted to ask him some questions, for which purpose it would be necessary for him to accompany them to the station. Not to catch a train, presumably.'

'Okay, but he hasn't been arrested. Not yet, at any rate. When and where did this happen?'

'Here, at the flat, at lunch time. He always tries to come home for lunch during the run. I'm usually still asleep when he leaves in the morning and at the theatre when he comes back, so it's about the only chance we get to meet.'

'Yes, all right, but what I really want to know is, did they just barge in and announce this out of the blue, or had there been a lot of leading up to it?'

'Not them. They'd already been through what I suppose you'd call the lead up when they came the first time. That was

57

at about nine o'clock this morning. Listen I'd find all this much easier to explain if you were here and I'll go raving mad if I have to stick it out on my own much longer. Can't you come round?'

'You know very well I can't. I have to be at the theatre in an hour's time and so do you. I suppose the show must go on, even if it kills us.'

'All right, then be a friend and get there early, will you? Leave now, this minute, and I'll do the same.'

I was unable to obey these instructions to the letter because the first necessity was to get hold of Robin. One of the few mitigating circumstances surrounding Dolly's death was that, whatever else, her attacker had at least had the decency to perform the deed in the Metropolitan area. If she had been murdered at her home in the country, it would doubtless have been a different story and I should have been just as much in the dark as everyone else about the line the investigation was taking and the progress, if any, it had led to. As it was, I could at least rely on Robin to keep me abreast of developments, to some extent and, by another stroke of fortune, he was alone in his office when I telephoned and able to lend at least one ear for about ninety seconds. He promised to do what he could and to let me know what success he had met with when he called for me after the show.

So then I went back up to the first-floor spare room again and told Philip that I was obliged to leave early, but that Robin would be back soon after seven. He told me not to worry, as he would be able to manage on his own for an hour or two. As there was a decanter of whisky and a telephone on the table beside him and a television set at the foot of the bed, to which his eyes were constantly straying as we spoke, I had no difficulty in believing him.

It struck me as I toiled downstairs again that he certainly possessed the most remarkable resilience in adversity, although, for the fifteenth time, was unable to decide whether or not this unnatural composure indicated that he really was entering his second childhood and was incapable of taking in what had happened and what it must inevitably mean for his future.

III

Half an hour later Clarrie was saying: 'Like I told you, the first time they came was about nine o'clock. At least, one of them did. I wasn't up, but Pete let him in and when they'd talked for a bit he asked to see me.'

I noticed that she was experiencing something less than her usual difficulty in remembering her loved one's name and wondered whether the enormity of the trouble he was in had somehow conferred a distinction on him, setting him apart from the other men in her life.

I said: 'What did he want to know?'

'Oh, things like when I'd last seen her ladyship, whether she'd seemed worried or nervous and so on and so forth. He gabbled on about how it was just a routine check and they were trying to get in touch with everyone who'd been in recent contact with her. Didn't they put you through the same treatment?'

'No.'

'Caesar's wife being above suspicion, I presume?'

'Not at all. What you forget is that they were swarming round our house in their hordes yesterday morning, as soon as Philip was declared to be strong enough to talk to them. They know how to get hold of me any minute they want to. Another thing you have to remember, Clarrie, is that they'll have checked up on all Dolly's movements during the few days before she was killed and they're bound to have discovered by now that you invited her and Philip to lunch at the cottage last Sunday. That would naturally give them the idea that you were on a special footing with her.'

'It would be the wrong idea. I loathed the sight of her.'

'I trust you didn't mention that?'

'No, of course not, and the point is it wasn't me who invited the Mickletons to lunch, it was that silly . . .'

'Exactly! And they'll probably want to know why. Still, we haven't got all night to argue about it. Get on with your story! How long did this personage spend at the flat?'

'About half an hour, I suppose. It was a nuisance because it made Pete late for work yet again, but at least he had a good excuse, for once. I'd practically forgotten all about it and then, just as we were tucking into our bread and cheese, in he marches again and this time he had a friend with him. That one said something about some new evidence having come to light which they thought Pete could give them some more information about and that it would simplify things if he would go along to the station with them. Don't you find that highly peculiar?'

'Not if they wanted him to look at some photographs, or something of that nature. And there were no charges or cautions?'

'No . . . no, not as far as I recall, but listen, Tessa, what can it mean? What could he possibly be able to tell them that would take all this time? Are they trying to bully him into confessing that he murdered the dreary woman, or something? But why pick on him? When he still hadn't come back after two hours I started falling apart. I rang the shop, of course, in case it had slipped his mind that I was still alive, but he wasn't there. Then I tried to get hold of my solicitor, but his secretary told me he was in court all day. Not that he'd probably have been the slightest use. Divorce is about the only thing he's had any experience of. Then I thought of you. I thought if anyone could help it bloody well ought to be you.'

'Well, I've alerted Robin and he's promised to do what he can. He'll be round later on and you can talk to him yourself,

60

but in the meantime there's something I want to ask you. Was there, on either occasion when they called at your flat, any mention of the anonymous letters?'

'No, there wasn't. What do you want to know that for?'

'Because, as far as we can make out, no one has mentioned them, not even Philip, which seems rather strange.'

'I don't see why. They were sent to him, not to her, and he's still alive, as far as anyone can tell, so what's the connection?'

'Oh, come on, you're losing your grip, aren't you? We all assumed they were meant for him, but we must have got it wrong, surely? No one was addressed by name and they weren't in envelopes, simply messages propped up on his shelf, where Dolly was just as sure to see them as he was. Isn't it more likely that she was the one who was being threatened? And supposing, for some reason which they kept to themselves, they both realised this at the time, wouldn't that account for her being in such a panic when he remained so calm? It's much easier to dismiss these things as a joke when you're not directly concerned, rather more difficult to laugh it off if you happen to be the one who's under attack.'

'But if Philip knew, or had guessed the letters were for her, why didn't he tell the police about them when she was killed?'

'Possibly because he now feels remorseful and ashamed for having made light of them and, being the vain fellow he is, he doesn't want to admit it.'

'Why don't you ask him?'

'I mean to, when I find the right moment, although it may not be necessay now.'

'And, in any case, I can't see what it has to do with Pete.'

'Well, you see, Clarrie, the question is, did the police know from the beginning about the letters, or have they just found out and the reason why he's been hauled off like this is because they've got the idea that if they coax him a bit he may be able to come up with some suggestions about who might have sent them.'

'Then it'll be a waste of coax. How could he possibly . . . God Almighty, Tessa, you wouldn't be hinting that he'd put them together himself, would you?'

As it happened, the thought had occurred to me, since there was a combination of slyness and impudence about the letters themselves and the manner of their delivery, characteristics which I also associated with Pete. However, this was hardly a suitable audience to try out such theories on, so I said: 'No, of course not. All I suggested was that he might possess some knowledge, while having no idea of its relevance, which the rest of us don't. After all, he and Dolly were two of a kind, in a sense.'

'Oh, nicely put, I must say!'

'Not in the sense of being alike, but because of both being on the fringes of the action. They were spectators, in a manner of speaking and for that reason may have seen more of the game than those of us who were taking part in it. If it was a fact that Dolly had realised that the letters were intended for her and had either found out or guessed who was sending them, why should not Pete have also guessed or found out?'

'Then he'd have told me, wouldn't he?'

'That would depend.'

'On what?'

'On the identity of Anon, partly; but also on how he'd got hold of the information. Say Dolly had told him and then sworn him to secrecy, for fear of its getting back to Philip and demoralising him completely?'

'I still don't see why it should be necessary for the poor boy to spend hours and hours being questioned about it. If he really knows something of that kind it wouldn't take him five minutes to pass it on.'

'Unless he's decided not to co-operate. In other words, is protecting someone who is more important to him than Dolly was. Anyway,' I added hurriedly before she could ask me who that might be, 'I could easily be wrong. I'm only trying to make you understand that there can be circumstances where someone is put through a long interrogation, without having committed any crime or being suspected of any, and therefore that you may not have anything at all to worry about.'

'Well, it sounds highly dubious to me, but you're the expert, so I suppose I'll have to take your word for it.'

It was a relief to know that she had rather more faith in my word than I had myself, for although I believed some of what I had told her to be reasonably plausible, I was privately of the opinion that there must be more to it than that. However, the object had been to build her up into a fit state of mind to get through the evening performance and, since this now appeared to have been achieved, I left her to dress, trusting that nothing would occur to undo the good work at least until after the final curtain.

It was touch and go because when Robin arrived in my dressing room just before the interval and gave me the latest news, I became so petrified that Clarrie would come bursting in and drag it out of him that I implored him to go away at once and return in an hour's time, to assist in the mopping-up operation.

CHAPTER SEVEN

At seven o'clock, after five and a half hours of close interrogation, Pete was allowed to go home, although he did not do so without a stain on his character. Indeed, all things considered, he was lucky to have escaped arrest on charges of conspiracy to murder.

This fate, in fact, might still be awaiting him, although I had been wrong in supposing that the evidence against him was in any way connected with the anonymous letters, being based on a potentially far more damaging incident.

The early morning police call, as described by Clarrie, had been little more than a formality, since at that time there had been no reason to link the murder with people or events at the theatre. Unfortunately for Pete, though, the constable concerned had been an alert and observant young man who had immediately recognised something familiar about his witness, although maintaining a discreet silence on this point and continuing to conduct the business on casual, non-commital lines until he had consulted his superior officer, who had then accompanied him on the lunch time call at the flat.

'But what could he have recognised as familiar about him?' I asked Robin. 'I don't understand.'

'In the sense of his striking resemblance to a description that had been circulated to everyone working on the case. It was the single shred of firm evidence which had so far come in and they'd got it from the woman who occupied the flat next door to the Mickletons, the very one, in fact, where Philip had gone for help when he found his wife had been murdered.'

'Meaning that she saw a young man who looked exactly

like Pete coming out of the next door flat between six and six-thirty yesterday evening?'

'Not coming out, going in, and it wasn't between six and six-thirty. If it had been, they wouldn't now have turned him loose.'

'At what time then?'

'About three hours later. She was on her way home from a bridge party and she saw this young man standing outside the Mickletons' front door, with the key in the lock.'

'Did she speak to him, ask him what he was doing there?'

'There was no need. He looked round when he heard her coming and said good evening. She said good evening back and he then volunteered the information that Lady Mickleton had sent him to collect something she needed urgently and to take it to the theatre for her.'

'Well, that doesn't sound like a man planning to commit murder, which in any case he couldn't have been since she was already dead, so what's the problem?'

'One theory is that either he, or someone he's in collusion with, had been there at the earlier time, when the neighbour was out at her bridge and then, as the evening wore on, had become obsessed by the fear of having left some incriminating evidence behind, like finger prints on a door knob, or something of that kind. You know how it can happen to the best of us? However often you tell yourself that you didn't leave the gas on, you still feel the compulsion to go back and make sure.'

'But the only thing they have to go on is this woman's description?'

'It's pretty damning, close enough, anyhow, for P.C. Blair to have made the connection and this afternoon when they put him into an identity parade, she picked him out with no hesitation at all. I know that's not proof, but it's not a point in his favour either.'

'And does this tiresome Mrs Bridge Player know how long

he spent in the next door flat?'

'Oh, indeed, almost to the second. She admitted that he hadn't been furtive or fazed in any way when he spoke to her, but she said that people have cheek enough for anything these days and, being very burglar-conscious, she wasn't entirely satisfied with his explanation. She left her own front door open an inch or two and waited to see what would happen. Her plan was to give it five minutes and then, if he hadn't emerged, to dial 999.'

'But he beat her to it?'

'By all of two minutes, in fact. He wasn't carrying anything when he came out, but, as she admitted, if it had been a piece of jewellery, or powder compact, or something of that kind, it would have been natural to put it in his pocket. Anyway, so far as she was concerned, it proved that he either hadn't gone there with evil intent,or that she'd succeeded in scaring him off. So her own conscience was clear and she made herself a hot drink, went to bed and forgot all about it until a couple of hours later when the balloon went up.'

'And, presumably, Pete denies that he was there at all?'

'Over and over again. Nothing will shake him. His story, which he has stuck to from the beginning, is the same as he told you and me and Clarrie. He'd bought her a present in the morning, remembered at the crucial moment that he'd left it at the shop and got held up in a traffic jam when he went back to fetch it. It's rather a heavy coincidence that all this should have taken place during the period when his identical twin was letting himself into the Mickleton's flat.'

'And how did your boys come to hear that he was absent during that very period? I didn't tell them and I don't think it's likely that Clarrie did either. Not you, by any chance?'

'No, but as it happens you and I weren't the only two people she was screeching and moaning about it to. Hartman got a dose of it as well.'

'Hartman?'

'Isn't that the name of Oliver Welles' partner?'

'Yes, yes, of course it is, Benjie Hartman, but how does he come into it?'

'By going round after the show to congratulate her.'

'And she ranted on about Pete leaving her high and dry?'

'Not being the soul of reticence, as we know. And so when it came to his turn to go through the business of accounting for his movements yesterday evening he remembered to include a graphic description of that episode too. One shouldn't blame him. He was only concerned with producing as many witnesses as he could lay his hands on to back up his own story and he couldn't have known what a bonus he was throwing in.'

'But I still think there must be some mistake. After all, he really had bought Clarrie a present, you know. She showed it to me the next morning. It was a gold watch.'

'Leaving aside the fact that it could have been in his pocket all the time, instead of at the shop, as he insists, I have a nasty feeling that the present, in itself, could count as a mark against him, if it were to be used in evidence, as he is probably all too well aware. I daresay he has quoted the price for it which was less than half the actual cost.'

'Why would he do that and what bearing could it have on Dolly's murder?'

'Not a direct one, but a bearing, nonetheless. You see, I haven't told you the worst of it yet. It seems he has some form.'

'Been in jug, in other words?'

'You take it calmly. I had expected that to be the worst shock of all.'

'I don't know whether I've gone beyond being shocked,' I admitted, 'or whether that bit seemed to fit so smoothly into place. I'd always thought he must have been trained as a dancer at some point in his life. All those darting movements conjured up pictures of someone leaping about in tights, with a tinkling piano in the background, but I suppose a training in cat burglary, with a lot of thugs in the background would do just as well. Is that what he was in for?'

'Not far off, although to be fair, it was some years ago and he was only a callow youth at the time. He got in with a gang of much older boys and they brought off a series of break-ins in a plushy, residential suburb close to where he lived. They got away with half a dozen quite sizeable jobs before they were nicked.'

'What did he get?'

'Two years in Borstal.'

'Since when he has turned over a new leaf?'

'That remains to be seen. It's another of those awkward questions. He's certainly had no convictions since then, but that may be due more to luck than good behaviour. He appears to enjoy a somewhat more opulent life style than one would have thought possible on the salary from an antique shop.'

'I don't see why. It's a very grand and expensive shop and, apart from his salary, he probably gets commission on everything he sells. Also I don't doubt that Clarrie contributes her whack to the upkeep of the life style.'

'Like paying for the gold watch he gives her as a first night present, for example?'

'Yes, well, okay, so they're trying to make out he's a fence, or something?'

'Not as far as I know. In fact, it's quite likely he's not directly involved in any criminal activity, but a lot of the buying in his sort of business is done on a private basis. He'd automatically have amassed a store of inside knowledge about where the stock came from in the first place, as well as the lay-out of the houses and such other valuable items the owners might possess which aren't on the market, and he may also have retained enough contacts to be in a position to pass on such knowledge to various interested parties.'

'A kind of burglars' information service?'

'Something of the sort. At any rate, that's the line they're working on at present; seeing whether they can trace any link and, if they succeed, I'm afraid things will look pretty black for him. You doubtless consider it immoral and unfair that people's past misdemeanours should be held against them, but unfortunately that's how life is.'

'I still don't see what it has to do with Dolly's murder. Do they take the theory a stage further and suggest he killed her because she'd found about these shady goings-on and was threatening to turn him in?'

'I'm afraid they regard that as a possibility.'

'Rather a drastic way out of the problem, wasn't it?'

'But conceivable, you'd agree?'

'I'm not so sure that I would. In the first place, I don't see him acting in a violent way, unless it was in self-defence, when I am sure he could be very effective. Mischief-making, and cunning too, is more how I see him and something tells me that he'd have been capable of running enough rings round Dolly not to have to resort to anything so chancy as murder. Furthermore, it takes no account of the anonymous letters, which must somehow have a connection somewhere. I can see Pete as the mastermind behind that enterprise, that fits all right, but not as the one who undertook all the fiddling tedium of compiling them. That seems out of character too. Which reminds me, Robin, do you happen to know what became of those letters?'

'No, I have yet to hear a single mention of them.'

'Even from Philip?'

'Certainly not from Philip.'

'Which is strange, isn't it? It must have occurred to him by now that they were meant for Dolly and not for himself and therefore were probably sent by her murderer. You'd think he would have realised how important they could be as evidence?'

'Perhaps you ought to point it out to him?'

'Someone else suggested that, but why don't you?'

'Oh, I think it would come better from you. However hard I tried to explain that I was only out to give friendly, unofficial advice, there's no chance he'd believe me and that could lead to a whole series of apple carts being upset.'

'All right, I'll do it then; although I'll need to choose my moment carefully. He's so touchy these days, worse than ever. The mere mention of Dolly and he either starts to cry or says in a pained voice that he doesn't wish to discuss it. If it weren't for the fact that I don't believe him to be competent to commit a murder, I'd begin to think he had a guilty conscience.'

'That might not be bad,' Robin said, brightening at the thought. 'He'd get off gaol on medical grounds and he'd be well looked after in the psychiactric block and you and I could have our spare room back.'

CHAPTER EIGHT

'How can you expect me to be able to tell you a thing like that?' he asked, something approaching the right moment having arrived when I handed him his first ration of whisky the following evening. It was early for this, even by his standards, but he had arrived downstairs soon after five o'clock in his dressing gown, saying that he felt well enough to leave his room for an hour or two, and I was naturally anxious to reward and encourage any signs of returning mobility.

'But Philip, surely you must remember?' I protested. 'Do please at least try! Can't you see what a help those letters could be in finding out who did this dreadful thing?'

'In that case, it's a pity you advised me to tear one of them up.'

'Oh, so you do remember that much? Well, we seem to be getting somewhere. How about the others?'

'My dear child, there's nothing wrong with my memory. The point is, I'd given them to Dolly.'

'All three?'

'Yes. After you'd shown the first two to Robin she said she was going to take charge of those and any more that came and lock them up in a safe place. That's what she said and presumably that's what she did.'

'It must have been not only a very safe place but a very inaccessible one too, because so far they haven't been found.'

'I expect they're in her jewel case, if you really want to know.'

'But, Philip, didn't the police ask you for the keys to all that sort of thing?'

'How can you expect me to remem . . . yes, yes, of course they did.'

'Of course they did, and you may be sure they made good use of them. They'll have gone through every item she possessed with a toothcomb, looking for some clue to the murderer's identity. Did they ask your permission to search the Old Rectory too?'

'Oh, er, yes, now you mention it.'

'So there we are! Obviously, the letters were neither at the flat nor in the country, otherwise we'd have heard about it by now. So what could she have done with them?'

'Really, Tessa, I don't see what right you have to keep nagging me like this. People never stop going on and on at me and I'm getting absolutely sick of it.'

'Yes, I know and I'm sorry, but I should have thought it might upset you even more to know that someone had killed her and got away with it.'

'Knowing who did it won't bring her back,' he said, starting to snivel.

I resigned myself then to accepting that he either knew nothing and cared less about what had become of the letters, or knew and cared enough to use every trick in his somewhat limited repertoire to keep the knowledge to himself. Either way, I was wasting my time, so I topped up his drink, to atone for my lack of sensitivity and changed the subject, reminding him that I should soon have to be on my way to the theatre for the final performance of *Elders and Betters*.

'Sooner you than me,' he said indifferently. 'I'd prefer to put every single memory of that godforsaken play out of my head and never have to think of it again.'

'Understandable, and I can't say it's had a lot of happy moments for any of us. I think that must be why Oliver's giving his party tonight.'

'Oliver? Giving a party, did you say?'

'Yes, at his house. It seems rather macabre, when we have so little to celebrate, but that's Oliver, always so thoughtful and kind. I'm sure the intention is to give us a tiny bang to go

72

out with, instead of whimpers all the way. It's really sweet of him, considering he's been the chief loser in the game.'

'Why haven't I been invited?'

'Oh, Philip, honestly! What a question! For one thing, you're not nearly well enough and, for another, I imagine it didn't occur to him that you'd be in a party mood.'

'No, I'm not and, in the circumstances, I consider it extremely bad taste to give one at all.'

He had drifted back into petulance and once again he had me floored. If my life had depended on it, I could not have sworn whether it was the death of his beloved wife that distressed him most at that moment, or simply the thought of missing a party, although not assuming him to be so witless as to play the hand in quite this way, if he had been the one to kill her.

II

Clarrie and I went together and, like most of the guests who had not been to Oliver's house before, we arrived later than we had intended.

It was one of four, tucked away behind the King's Road and evidently converted from the stables of a large private house. It was approached from a side street by an archway, just wide enough for the passage of a car, which opened out into a yard, surrounded by high walls on three sides, and our driver went past the entrance twice without recognising it for what it was. There were few pedestrians about at that hour and none of the first three we appealed to had so much as heard of Martingale Close. He had almost convinced us that no such address existed when we were rescued by a woman who stepped out of a taxi which had pulled up in front of ours, who informed us that she lived there herself and that it was practically staring us in the face.

None of this had done anything to improve Clarrie's

temper, which was a pity because it needed all the improvement it could get. The principal complaint was that Pete had not been invited. Space, we had been told, was limited and the invitations restricted to Tim, our director; Natalie Corcoran, the designer; John Somers who was in charge of the lighting; and members of the cast. This, with Oliver and Benjie, added up to the ominous total of thirteen.

'I nearly decided not to come,' she told me, 'but then I thought Oliver would imagine I was in a huff or something, so I told Pete I'd just put in an appearance for ten minutes. He didn't take it at all well.'

'Well, we needn't hang about. An appearance is what I'll be putting in myself, seeing that Robin wasn't invited either. We can make an excuse to leave early.'

'You can do as you like. Personally, I mean to make a night of it, given half a chance. When I said he didn't take it very well, it was an understatement.'

'Oh, dear! Does that mean you've had another quarrel?'

'Certainly not. I'm the most tolerant of women, as you know and no-one understands better than I do what a horrible time he's been through. I told him he had my deepest sympathy and I should make it my business to be home within the hour.'

'In that case, why are you now proposing to make a night of it?'

'Because the little blighter has gone flouncing off to the country in a tantrum. The excuse was that he wanted to go ahead of me and get the cottage cleaned up and shipshape for my arrival, but I can recognise sulking when I see it. I might add that none of this shipshape business has been necessary in the past and it's a long time since I saw him with a dishcloth in his hand.'

'He may want to be on his own for a bit. You ought to make allowances, you know, Clarrie.'

'I do make allowances. No-one makes more of them than I

74

do. I've told him I shan't be down till quite late tomorrow, so he can have a nice lie-in and still have time for the shipshape. Oh, hello darling!' she added, addressing the red-haired young man who was hovering on the cobblestones outside an open front door, 'Are you looking for someone?'

'Only you', he replied, kissing her warmly 'Oh, and you've brought Tessa! How nice to see you, Tessa!'

'You too, Benjie!'

By midnight, some of the guests were leaving, though none going in my direction and Clarrie was not among them. It was clear that her threat of making a night of it had not been idle chatter and she was getting all the encouragement she needed from Benjie. They had been swaying about on the dance floor, arms entwined round each other's necks, for what seemed like hours and the last thing she needed was someone to see her home, so I asked Oliver if he would telephone for a taxi. He said it was such a difficult place to find that most taxi drivers gave up in disgust and that, if I did not mind walking a few hundred yards, he would escort me to the King's Road, where we should find dozens of empty cabs, with drivers eager to do our bidding.

'I'm really surprised by Clarrie,' was his opening remark, as we strolled across the cobbled yard.

'I'd have thought you'd be used to her by now?'

'Oh, I'm not referring to her behaviour, though I do confess to finding that faintly distasteful, in the circumstances. Admittedly, Benjie is just as bad, if not worse, but he doesn't normally behave like this and at least he has the dubious excuse of being more than somewhat drunk. You were all so late arriving and the truth is that he was already becoming slightly incoherent before the party started. No, what really surprises me about Clarrie is that she came at all. I had to invite her, or she might have misunderstood, but I never dreamt she'd turn up.'

'She was afraid of offending you, just as you were afraid of offending her.'

'Oh, do you believe that? She must have known I shouldn't have been in the least offended. On the contrary, I find it quite inexplicable that she should have abandoned her young man at a time like this, in order to fling herself into the waiting arms of another one. Incidentally, Tessa, do you happen to know what that business with Pete was all about? She told me he'd been kept under lock and key for a whole day, but she'd no idea why, and he either didn't know himself, or wasn't telling. Don't you find that slightly incredible?'

'She does tend to exaggerate, you know; but I agree with you, it doesn't quite ring true. I am sure he does know, and isn't telling.'

'I wondered if it could have anything to do with those anonymous letters?'

We had reached the King's Road by this time, with not a cruising taxi in sight in either direction, but since the conversation had taken an interesting turn, which I now suspected to have been the object of our excursion, I was ready to fall in with his proposal that we should plod on to Sloane Square.

'Apparently not,' I replied.

'Ah! So you do know all about it?'

'By no means all, but I gather they've got hold of the idea that Pete possesses some vital information which, for reasons known only to himself, he has refused to part with, but Robin told me there'd been no mention of the letters. Philip says he gave them to Dolly, who intended to lock them away in a safe place, but she can't have done so, otherwise they'd have turned up by now. She must have changed her mind and burnt them.'

'I doubt that, you know. In fact, I'd stake my life on it that she kept them.'

'Is that your intuition speaking, Oliver, or do you know it for a fact?'

'A bit of both, perhaps. She told me she'd found out about the fourth letter because Philip, in his cups, had let it out and also that he'd been idiotic enough to throw it away. She was therefore going to hold me to my promise. She would give me until ten o'clock the next morning to call in the police, failing which she would personally take the other three letters to Scotland Yard and place them in the hands of the Assistant Commissioner, who, as I do not need to tell you, was an intimate friend.'

'I see! And when did this conversation take place? Or don't you need to tell me that either?'

'Apparently not. As you've evidently guessed, it was approximately eight hours before her death.'

'Had you told anyone else?'

'Only Benjie, who I considered had a right to know. Puts me in a rather dicey situation, wouldn't you say?'

'Oh, I don't know. Benjie could have put it around all over the place. He's not so discreet as you and, besides, I don't see you committing acts of violence. At any rate, not for such a poor motive as that one.'

'Why not?'

'Well, admittedly, it wouldn't have boded much good for your all-important first night to have the police stumping around backstage, looking for an anonymous letter writer, but on the other hand . . .'

'The death by strangulation of the leading man's wife would hardly have seemed a very bright alternative?'

'Exactly!'

'As a matter of fact, I did beg her on my knees to put off taking any action, at least until after we'd opened.'

'And she refused, of course; although it's hard to see why. She must really have had a fixation about this Anon meaning business to have become so single-minded about it, because, on the face of it, she and Philip had more to lose than anyone if the play flopped. Apart from yourself, that is.'

77

'There you are, you see! You've put it into words. I had the strongest motive of anyone for wanting to shut her up.'

'What are you trying to do, Oliver? Convince me that you're guilty?'

'On the contrary, I am trusting that, by being so free, frank and forthright in making out a case against myself, I shall convince you of my innocence.'

He had not made a bad job of it either, in my opinion, for I could not believe that he would have introduced the subject of the anonymous letters in the first place if he had had any hand in their disappearance. Nor had he neglected to draw my attention, in his free, frank and forthright fashion, to the fact that their coming to the attention of the public would have been far less damaging to his prospects than the murder of Dolly Mickleton.

CHAPTER NINE

I

On Sunday morning I received what was rapidly becoming the regular daily telephone call from Clarrie.

'Did you hear what happened after you left last night, Tessa?'

'No, but I can guess.'

'Oho, very humorous! And quite wrong too. The party ended somewhat differently from the way I, at any rate, had anticipated. Mainly your fault, as usual.'

'Why? What did I do this time?'

'Sneaking off like that and taking Godliness with you. You may be interested to hear that on the way home he got mugged.'

'Not just interested, but appalled. How awful, Clarrie! Where did it happen?'

'Practically on his own doorstep. Just inside the archway.'

'Was he much hurt?'

'Nothing to speak of. A few bruises and his nice clean suit all mussed up. It hadn't done his temper much good either.'

'Well, I should think not. How many of them set on him?'

'Only one, apparently, but he got away with the lot. Cash, credit cards, everything.'

'Oh, goodness, how awful! And you're right, I suppose it was partly my fault. I should have known he wouldn't be safe to walk home on his own. Poor old Oliver, he really is taking the knocks just now. And what a foul ending to his party!'

'Oh, indeed! Although I might tell you that it had become a right shambles long before the host came staggering back.'

'Oh, why? Had something else gone wrong?'

'Enough. It was really on account of his being away for such an age, so chalk that one up to yourself too, while you're at it. The booze had run out for a start and none of us poor hangers-on were sure whether we ought to drift away, or whether the civil thing would be to wait for the host to come back and be said goodbye to. The awful red-headed person was the worst of the lot.'

'Benjie?'

'That's the one.'

'What did he do?'

'Got very bellicose because he wanted a drink and, as the cupboard was locked, he couldn't get at it. Just as well, really, because he was already half-stoned, but the frustration had a terrible effect on him and he started telling everyone they'd better go home because it was quite obvious that Godliness didn't intend to come back and that you and he were most likely sitting in some booze parlour, laughing your rotten heads off. I tried to make him understand that nothing of that kind went on in your blameless little life, but he was past taking anything in.'

'And, quite apart from blameless me, it is hardly the kind of behaviour one associates with Oliver.'

'Well, he was drunk, you see, and it had reached the truculent stage. Finally, he announced that he was going home to open up his own bottle cupboard and, if anyone cared to accompany him, he'd be pleased to drive them there in two minutes flat in his dear old Jag, which was parked right outside. It wasn't a particularly inviting offer, the state he was in, so no-one took him up on it and off he flounced.'

'And then what?'

'That just left four weary old green bottles hanging on the wall, Tim, Natalie, me and Moody, who thought it would be beyond the pale to leave without saying cheery bye to the host, so we sat around for a bit, saying how ghastly it all was and how were we going to get home, and very lucky we did because we were still at it when he came staggering in. But for that, he'd have spent the night sobbing on the doorstep.'

'His keys had been snatched too?'

'I told you, everything he had on him. That was bad news because it meant we still couldn't get at the drink. I always think there must be something desperately untrustworthy about people who lock things up. Anyway, Godliness wasn't bothered at all about us, all he cared about was getting the locks changed and he kept moaning on about how he'd never find anyone to do the job on Sunday. So I suppose the poor wretch is having to spend the next twenty-four hours at home, guarding his property.'

'Well, at least that's one way I may be able to compensate. I'm sure Robin can use his influence to press some local locksmith into service. I'll go to work on it right away.'

'Yes, do, but before you hang up on me, Tessa, when will I see you? I'm going to the cottage in a minute, but I don't know how long I'll be staying. Pete proposes to take a few days off from work, but they're not going to be very halcyon days for me, unless the mood has changed since our last meeting. How about you? Any plans?'

'This afternoon we have to drive Philip down to his Old Rectory. They say he's well enough to manage on his own now and he's got faithful Mrs Gale, who's spent the last twenty years being bossed around by Dolly, to come in every day, so he should be all right. Shopping may be a slight problem because he doesn't drive any more, but we're hoping that some of the neighbours will rally there.'

'So you won't have to stay?'

'No, but I won't be far off, if he should run into a crisis. After we've dropped him, Robin and I are going to spend the night at Roakes with Toby. At least, it'll only be a one-night stop for Robin. I might stay on a bit longer.'

'Oh good! Then you won't be far away from me either, if I

should run into a crisis.'

'Believe it or not, that wasn't what influenced me. The inquest is tomorrow, you see. It'll only take ten minutes, then there'll be an adjournment and Philip has been let off on medical grounds, but there's the funeral to be got through on Tuesday. It's in their church just the other side of the garden hedge, so he'd have no excuse for not turning up at that and I suppose I'll have to, as well.'

'Well, don't expect me to accompany you. I haven't set foot inside a church for ten years and her ladyship would be the last one to break that tradition.'

II

Less than an hour later I was able to telephone Oliver and tell him that help was at hand in the matter of lock changing. He thanked me politely, but people are rarely so ecstatically grateful for these small, but time-consuming services as they ought to be and he was no exception. He seemed less concerned with what I had done than with what I had left undone.

'I'm afraid you're being a little optimistic in saying this man can be here by twelve, Tessa dear. I rather wish you'd let me speak to him myself. I don't doubt for a minute that you gave him the right directions, but I am sorry to tell you that it probably won't be enough. People have the utmost difficulty in finding their way. I've often had to wait in for a whole morning for someone who said he'd be here at ten and when they do turn up they're invariably in a foul temper and bungle the job, to pay me out for living in such an inaccessible place.'

'Have no fear, Oliver! All that has been anticipated and taken care of. Mr Barksfield's premises are just around the corner from us and he will call here on his way. I shall then accompany him personally to your place of residence, okay? I felt it was the least I could do,' I added, shovelling on a few coals of fire, 'since it was on my account that you have been plunged into this sea of troubles.'

This brought him up sharp, he became quite humble in his expression of gratitude and indebtedness and, by the time Mr Barksfield and I presented ourselves on the appointed dot, he was abject in his apologies as well. This was only natural, for it had then become as close to a case of shutting the stable door after the horse had left as I had ever come across.

'Sheer, utter madness and I'm entirely to blame this time. I could kick myself now, but who would have dreamt it could happen so quickly?'

'How long were you away?'

'Oh, ten minutes. Not more than fifteen at the most. I just nipped down the road to get the Sunday papers. They close at twelve and I suppose the mere fact of knowing that help was on the way took me off my guard.'

'And when you got back was there anyone in the yard?'

'Not a soul. Just one or two parked cars, as usual. He must have been waiting and watching for his chance and I daresay he was in and out of the place before I'd got as far as the newsagents. I guessed immediately what had happened because I could see from twenty yards away that the front door was open.'

'Are you sure you hadn't gone so far off your guard that you forgot to shut it?'

'Oh no, Tessa, someone was here all right, no question about it. The carriage clock has gone from this room and a rather nice little bronze, as well as my best bits of silver from the sideboard.'

'So quite a discriminating thief?'

'It would appear.'

'Have you rung the police?'

'About twenty minutes ago. They promised to send someone round immediately, but that's still well below the average.'

'Then you'd better make a complete list of what's missing. That's the first thing they'll want.'

'There's nothing else, so far as I can tell,' he said, taking off his spectacles to give them a polish with his clean white handkerchief and so causing me to wonder why the advice should have embarrassed him.

'And another thing they'll want to know, Oliver, is everything you can tell them about the mugging, whether you can give any description of the man who attacked you.'

'Not a chance. He came at me from behind and knocked me to the ground. I think I must have passed out for a minute or two, from shock or fright or something. When I came to, he'd gone and so had my money, keys and credit cards.'

'And something else as well, presumably?'

'Not that I know of. What makes you say so?'

'Well, you must have been carrying something which had your address on it. Otherwise, how would he have known which front door the keys fitted?'

'Yes . . . yes, you're right, of course. How odd! I never thought of it. Thank you for reminding me. There must have been something and I'll have to try and think what it could have been. A letter perhaps?'

'Or did he know exactly who you were and where you lived?'

'You mean some local chap who's seen me going in and out? Yes, that's a thought. Oh, do forgive me, Tessa! I'm not being very hospitable, am I? Listen, why don't I ask your kind Mr Barksfield to forget about the front door for the moment and apply his skills to opening up the cupboard for us?'

'No, I think you should let him get on with the most important job and, anyway, I haven't really time for a drink. We're driving Philip to the country this afternoon.'

'Oh, really? What time will you be leaving?'

'After lunch. About three, I should think. We thought, if he had a decent lunch, he wouldn't need to bother much about dinner.'

'Dear Tessa, always so thoughtful!' Oliver remarked in an abstracted voice and not making it sound particularly complimentary.

I was on the point of saying goodbye when he spoke again: 'I was wondering . . . I'd hate to be a nuisance, but would it be all right if I were to look in for ten minutes later on, to say goodbye to the old boy?'

'Yes, of course. Come to lunch, if you get through here in time.'

'No, no, wouldn't dream of it. You have taken on quite enough already. It's just that I do feel I've been rather neglectful. I'll come about half past two, if I may and just say a few words.'

'Wouldn't you call that pushing good manners to extravagant lengths?' I asked Robin, who had been keeping an eye on the roast lamb, 'I can't see that he's been any more neglectful than anyone else. Rather less so, on the whole. He wrote Philip a marvellous letter. It was really beautifully expressed and quite uplifting. All written in his own immaculate hand, too. I hardly see why he feels it necessary to do more.'

'In other words, he is up to something?'

'You think so?'

'Oh no, not me, but I've noticed that when someone behaves in a way which you personally find abnormal, you always say that it's because they're up to something.'

'And experience has shown,' I replied, 'that most of them are.'

CHAPTER TEN

I

'And what is this one up to?' Toby asked at breakfast the next morning, Robin having set forth to London before either of us was awake.

'I never discovered. He arrived, according to plan, soon after half past two, when Philip was upstairs finishing off his packing. Oliver said that, rather than hold us up, he would go and talk to him there. They were together for about ten minutes, also according to plan. Then Philip came down and said that Oliver would be bringing the suitcase, but that he'd found it necessary to go to the spare bathroom first. So I'm none the wiser.'

'And you didn't just happen to be passing the door and happen to hear raised voices from inside?'

'Don't be ridiculous! In any case, I felt sure I could rely on Philip to pass on every word as soon as we were in the car.'

'But he didn't?'

'No. He either hadn't listened to anything Oliver said, or he'd forgotten what it was by then.'

'Or he's up to something too?'

'Wouldn't surprise me. I've scarcely known a time when he wasn't.'

'Though I suppose you wouldn't go so far as to say he was up to murdering his wife?'

'I wouldn't put it past him. He's quite unprincipled, as you know. The main thing that puts me off that idea is that it was such a funny time to have done it; just hours before the preview.'

'Also, as with all unprincipled people, myself included, self-interest is the guiding force and what possible advantage could her death have brought him? It is true that she was not a likeable woman, but they seemed to undestand each other and get along well enough. Furthermore, not even you would deny that she was a dedicated and devoted wife, if you care for that sort of thing. I cannot see one single way in which he is going to be better off without her.'

'I can, I can see several and the one which springs most readily to mind is that he'll be a lot better off financially. She was the one with all the money and, whether she made a will or not, the bulk of it is bound to go to him.'

'And since she managed her money very cleverly and never spent a penny that could be turned into twopence, what improvement will that make? So far as I can see, the only difference is that he will now have to sign the cheques.'

'Which is all the difference in the world.'

'Why? You surely don't suggest that she was about to leave him and run off with someone else? I consider that most unlikely. Even if the man could be found to exist who would take her on, you can't have forgotten how she revelled in being Lady Mickleton and basking in the reflection of such glory as still remained to him? I can't see her giving all that up just for a man. And allow me to remind you that, with or without one, under the present law, Philip would have been entitled to at least a third of her income, which I feel sure he would have had no hesitation in claiming, and that would not have appealed to her at all.'

'I agree with everything you say and I had never contemplated the possibility of her leaving him. Quite the other way round, in fact. It had occurred to me that he might have killed her for the simple reason that she was refusing to do so.'

'I thought it was agreed that he had no reason for wishing her to?'

'No, not quite. We've said what a dedicated and devoted

wife she was, which is true, but I can well imagine that there were times when he found her a damn sight too dedicated for his comfort. She was extremely shrewish and domineering, you know, nagging him from morning till night about taking his pills and not having another drink, so that he could hardly call his soul his own. All for his own good, no doubt, but he must have found it irksome sometimes, specially when she bossed him about in public. And it was going to get worse, you know, Toby. He must have realised that jobs would be growing scarce from now on, so that little escape route would be sealed off, in addition to which he would become more and more dependent on her for money.'

'Well, if you're right, I personally consider he acted too hastily. I really cannot see that life without her is going to be much fun.'

'The trouble is, you may underestimate him or at any rate underestimate his own opinion of himself. It would never surprise me if he had his eye on someone else.'

'Now I know you're joking. That is going too far.'

'No, it isn't. You find it ludicrous and I don't blame you, but Philip is terribly vain and I have a suspicion that he still likes to see himself as the great lover and God's gift to the female sex, specially now that he'll have a fat income to offer, as well.'

'Besides being so doddery that he can hardly crawl from one side of the stage to the other?'

'And there,' I announced, 'you have touched on a very interesting point.'

'I am so glad. It is the kind of thing I am always hoping to touch on, but it is not one which you had overlooked, I suppose?'

'Oh, indeed no, it's about the first thing one associates with Philip these days; but, you know, the strange thing is, Toby, that he only started to go downhill like this quite recently, during the last five or six weeks, in fact. As actors go, he's not all that old and he'd never have been engaged for such a demanding part if he'd projected the senile kind of image we're getting now. You could argue perhaps, and many people do accept it as reasonable, that the strain of taking over at short notice and half-way through rehearsals has been too much for him, but I'm not one of them.'

'Why is that?'

'Partly because, if nothing else, he is at least very experienced and he must have realised exactly what he was taking on; but mainly because of what happened on the first night. I'm prepared to concede that his collapse then was genuine, but the curious thing is that when he was removed by ambulance to Beacon Square and we called our own doctor in, he told us there was no cause for alarm. He said that Philip was as sound in wind and limb as most men of his age and that he'd be as fit as a fiddle after a few days' rest. All of which leads me to believe that he may have been faking some of this feebleness and that he's actually about twice the man he would have us believe him to be. Do you wish to hear what I suspect his game might be?'

'Not particularly.'

Ignoring this, as he had known I would, I said: 'In fact, Robin assures me that very little physical strength is needed to commit a murder of that kind. Providing you position yourself correctly, it's no more trouble than tying up a parcel and, of course, it's made simpler than ever if the victim has her back to you, best of all if she's asleep. By the time she realised what was happening it would be too late to do anything about it. However, assuming that Philip had had no previous experience of that type of thing, he may have been unaware of how like falling off a log it would turn out to be. So my theory is that, having planned to murder Dolly, he would quite naturally have sought to eliminate any risk of becoming the prime suspect. Hence his slide downhill over the past few weeks. He had a good thing going for him, in so far as he and

Dolly were known to be such a devoted couple and his intention was to consolidate his position by establishing in advance
that he lacked the physical strength to carry out such a deed.
Mind you, I'm not saying that this is a true picture of the
facts, only that it's feasible.'

'And it will be interesting to see whether you are right. If
so, I suppose we can look forward to a brisk rejuvenation
setting in. He will once more be striding through life with an
elastic step and a new little lady at his side.'

II

One little lady already at his side when I called at The Old
Rectory a few hours later, to deliver some groceries which he
had asked me to pick up in Storhampton, was Clarrie.

This was unexpected, but a relief too, for I had been a shade
worried when she did not keep her promise to telephone me
early on Monday morning. Despite loud protestations to the
contrary, I had been unable wholly to dismiss the possibility
of Pete being a murderer and, from time to time, had been
bothered by the thought of her spending the night alone with
him in their isolated cottage. I had consoled myself to some
extent with the reminder that few people in this world were
better equipped to look after themselves than she was and that
the most recent quarrel had now most likely burnt itself out
and they had already reached a state of truce and redeploy-
ment of forces for the next one.

Unhappily, this was not the case, as I discovered when she
followed me into the kitchen, where I was unpacking the
provisions, having put the bill in my pocket, on the remote
chance that Philip would show some curiosity about it.

I asked her what had brought her there and she replied:
'Oh, I don't know. I suppose there must be some tiny drop of
the Christian spirit still lurking in the wings, despite all my
efforts to eradicate it. It occurred to me that it must be rather

ghastly for the poor old knight, sitting here all alone while that grisly inquest was going on and everyone referring to her late ladyship as the cadaver and things like that. If I'd known you were coming, I'd probably have told the Christian spirit to take a running jump, but I didn't and I thought the gallant and noble thing would be to sail over and take his mind off things for a bit.'

'I bet you did that all right! But how did you get here, Clarrie? I didn't see any car outside. Did Pete bring you and then go away again?'

'Not Pete, the other one.'

'Which other one?'

'Old Redhead.'

'Benjie, you mean?'

'That's the one.'

'Honestly, Clarrie, all this switching about! You ought to be ashamed of yourself! No wonder you have such trouble remembering their names!'

'It's not exactly a trouble, but I'm apt to wander a bit sometimes and call them by the wrong one, which doesn't go down very well.'

'I suppose not, but tell me this: how does Benjie come to be driving you over here to see Philip this morning?'

'Quite simple, dear. I rang him up and asked him to. I knew he was spending part of the weekend with his parents because before he got so tiresome and drunk at that terrible party he told me so and offered me a lift as far as the cottage.'

'And so this morning you rang him up and commanded him to come all the way back to the cottage, in order to take you to call on Philip, which he obligingly did?'

'You're so quick on the uptake, Tessa, I do admire it. To be precise, he said it would suit him very well, because he was on the point of leaving anyway and, if I didn't need to spend too long cheering Philip up, he'd loiter about at the pub for half an hour and then drive me on to London.'

'I am the last one to jump to hasty conclusions, but it does begin to sound as though you hadn't made up your quarrel with Pete yet?'

'Not a chance. Unfortunately, it takes two to make up a quarrel.'

'And he wasn't co-operating?'

'He wasn't there. Not when I arrived, that is. I got an early train, you see, the ten fifty, which cost me a formidable effort, I might add, but I was feeling a touch remorseful, by then. Also I'd got to bed earlier than I'd expected and, one way and another, it seemed like a good idea. All the same, it was a fearful scramble and, by the time I'd finished talking to you, I realised that the only way I could ring him up and tell him what train I'd be on was by missing it, so I waited till I got to Dedley and guess what?'

'No reply?'

'You're so quick! At that point I nearly rang you up and asked you to send Robin over to collect me, but I wasn't sure I could rely on you to pass on the message. In the end I got a taxi up, which cost me about half last week's salary, and when I got to the cottage he still wasn't there.'

'How terrible for you!'

'Yes, it was. His car wasn't there either, so I knew he hadn't just gone for a walk or down to the village. I felt quite ill with frustration. Wouldn't you have? All that effort and good intentions and then wham, bang, slap in the face. For two pins I'd have gone straight back to London, only I'd run out of money by that time and where do you cash a cheque on Sunday morning when you're surrounded by nothing but trees?'

'What time did he eventually get back?'

'Around four, I suppose,' Clarrie replied, absent-mindedly removing the top of the gin bottle, which had been one of the items on Philip's shopping list, and pouring herself a generous measure. 'Refused to say where he'd been, to add insult to injury. I am very tolerant, as you know, but that was a bit too much for anyone. So I stated my case, which took an hour or two, owing to frequent interruptions and, as the sun most definitely had gone down on my wrath, I got up early and telephoned the red-head and here I am.'

'And since you obviously won't be here for long and the purpose of your visit was the altruistic one of cheering up Philip, maybe you ought to put in a few minutes on that, while I get all this stuff packed away?'

'Whatever you say!' she replied and ambled away, still clutching the gin bottle.

'Clarrie was looking well,' I remarked, more for something to say than from any deep interest in the subject.

'Yes, very splendid. She's a glorious creature, but rather wearing. Talks too much.'

'Well, at least you didn't have to endure it for long. As far as I can make out, she was only here for about twenty minutes and she spent ten of them wearing me out in the kitchen.'

'That's not the same thing. You seem to forget what I'm going through.'

'No, I don't, but the inquest will be over by now. You must try and put it out of your mind.'

'Easy for you to talk,' he grumbled and then relapsed into silence again.

When it had begun to sit rather heavily on us, I said: 'There's nothing else worrying you, is there, Philip? Apart from the inquest, I mean, and missing Dolly so badly?'

'You don't consider that enough?'

'Oh, it would be for most people,' I agreed, seeing what a little flattery would do, 'a great deal more than enough, but up to now you've borne up so well, been so marvellously brave. I wondered why it should have hit you so badly now?'

'It was a different environment, easier to be detached then. Now that I'm back here in our old dear home, where we spent so many happy hours together and surrounded by all her beloved objects . . .'

The pathos of it, despite being laid on a trifle too thickly, was causing the tears to flow and I said hastily: 'Yes, of course, very foolish and unimaginative of me not to have foreseen that; but I suppose it had to be faced some time and the longer you put it off the worse it would have been.'

'I do wish you would stop talking in platitudes, Tessa. It's getting on my nerves.'

It was tempting to reply that nothing would have given me more pleasure than to stop talking in anything at all, to walk out of the house and leave him to wallow in his own self-pity, but that would not have brought the errand of mercy to a very satisfactory conclusion, so I said meekly: 'Okay, Philip, what would you like to talk about?'

'Nobody can understand what it's like . . . being alone and having to make decisions all the time . . . I'm very worried and I don't know what I should do.'

'About what, in particular?'

'I couldn't make up my mind whether to mention it or not. At first, I decided not to, but then I remembered how you nagged and pestered me about those anonymous letters, as though they must be important in some way. And, for all I know, there could be other people who know about this too, so sooner or later it might come out and then perhaps I'd be in trouble for suppressing evidence.'

'I'm finding this rather hard to follow, Philip. Are you telling me there's been another letter, by any chance?'

'No, no, certainly not. Way off the mark,'

'Then do please explain!'

'I can do better than that,' he said, getting up and walking over to the door, if not with an elastic step, with somewhat more spring than he had shown for several days. 'Come with me.'

He led the way to the morning room, which was at the

back of the house, overlooking the garden and just large enough to accommodate two swivel chairs, a filing cabinet and an enormous, executive type desk in the bay window, complete with blotter, pen tray, engagement diary and telephone.

Walking up to it and taking a small key from his pocket, he said: 'Dolly used this as her office. It was where she did all her accounts and correspondence. She was so business-like, you know. I never had to bother about a single thing after I married her, not so much as a Christmas card.'

The key fitted the left-hand bottom drawer and when he had pulled it open he stood back so that I could look at the contents. After such an elaborate build-up, it was disappointing to find they consisted simply of the materials she had needed for wrapping her parcels. There was a ball of string in one corner, a tube of glue in another, with three different sized pairs of scissors between them, on top of a stack of neatly folded, unused brown paper.

I stared at this collection for over a minute, before its significance hit me.

'Now look underneath,' Philip ordered me.

I obeyed and saw what I was now half prepared for, a pile of newspapers, also so neatly folded as to suggest that they had never been opened and had lain there untouched since they left the shop.

CHAPTER ELEVEN

'So tell me what you make of that,' I said, having described this dramatic incident to Toby.

'That she had gone right out of her odious mind, presumably.'

'It's one possibility. Would you care to hear what construction Philip puts on it?'

'If you think it would amuse me.'

'I couldn't swear to that, but you may find it interesting because it shows distinctly more insight and imagination than I had believed him to possess. His theory is that Dolly, correctly as it turns out, was convinced that someone meant to kill her. However, she did not know who it was, or not for certain anyway and, having no proof, she realised that no-one would believe such a melodramatic tale. They would put it down to hysteria, or change of life or something, so she devised this scheme of manufacturing the proof by sending herself anonymous letters.'

'The flaw in that argument being that nobody realised until it was too late that the letters were intended for her and not for Philip.'

'Exactly! And that was intentional on her part and what I find so shrewd of Philip to have understood. He believes that she did it deliberately, guessing that, if the letters had been addressed to her, no-one would have paid much attention. Whereas, if it looked as though Philip were being threatened, Oliver would be bound to call in the police, in order to protect his valuable star and potentially valuable production. He believes, and he must have known better than anyone how her mind worked, that she would have foreseen that they, being both impartial and experienced in such matters, would have had no fixed, preconceived ideas about who the letters were intended for and would have conducted their investigations accordingly. In other words, they would be looking not only for someone who had a grudge against Philip, but also for someone who had it in for Dolly, thereby scaring the wits out of whoever it was and bringing it home to them that there was a fat chance of murdering her and getting away with it. There's a certain twisted logic in it, you must agree, and it would explain why, right from the start she got so much more steamed up about the letters than anyone else and why she became so furious and frustrated when Oliver continued to be feeble and irresolute about taking any action.'

'Though you'd have thought that, if she really believed her life was in danger, she'd have mentioned it once or twice in passing, at least in the privacy of the boudoir?'

'Apparently, she didn't. At least, not in that connection, although Philip did tell me that she had suffered for years from hypochondria and got into a state over the most trifling symptoms. An ordinary bilious attack was enough to make her believe that she had been struck down by a fatal disease. I found that rather surprising, not the sort of neurosis one associated with extrovert Dolly, but it just shows how little one ever knows about what goes on in other people's lives. However, I count it as a point in Philip's favour that he doesn't claim that she went so far as to hint that someone was trying to kill her. It would have been one very obvious way to back up his version of how the letters came to be written, if he had invented the whole story for my benefit and planted the evidence in the little bottom drawer himself.'

'Why should he have bothered to do that?'

'To shut me up, is the only reason I can think of. Perhaps he knows there is a very different answer to the puzzle and wants to head me off it, or perhaps he feels remorseful and guilt-ridden now for having treated the letters so lightheartedly and realises that, if he had behaved more responsibly, Dolly might still be alive. So it is more satisfying to his vanity that the letters should be buried and forgotten and to that end he would fob me off with any old tale, just to stop me going on about it. I wouldn't put it past him, but I thought at first that the big snag there was that he couldn't have put the evidence together himself, simply because there hasn't been a single opportunity since her death to get his hands on it. Now I can see, of course, that it would hardly have presented any problem at all. It would have been typical of Dolly to have kept a handy supply of new brown paper for her parcels, instead of making do with bits and pieces of left-overs, like the rest of us. There's one thing I do regret, though, and that is that it didn't occur to me to sneak a look at the dates on those newspapers. If they'd been back numbers, it wouldn't have positively proved that his story of having found them in the drawer was true, but if just one of them had post-dated the murder it would have blown it to smithereens. Too late now, though.'

'Oh, surely you can invent some excuse to take another look next time you go visiting?'

'Unfortunately, when he asked me what I thought he should do about it, my brain wasn't working very fast and I said that, since a bundle of unopened newspapers would be useless as evidence and, if his understanding of their purpose was correct, the letters, should they ever by found, wouldn't provide any clue to the identity of her murderer, there was nothing to be gained by doing anything. He might just as well use them to light the fire. If some of them happened to bear the wrong date, you may be sure the last piece of advice was carried out within two minutes of my leaving the house.'

'Yes, he does seem to have cut the ground very neatly from under your feet. What a wily old person he is turning out to be!'

'Or else completely ingenuous and as baffled as the rest of

us. I don't see how I am ever going to find out which. And that's not the only bother because now we come to the puzzling behaviour of Mr Oliver Welles.'

'Oh, do we really? Have you no mercy?'

'But don't you find it altogether mysterious, Toby? It's another thing I can't make up my mind about, whether to believe that mugging story or not.'

'My dear girl, why should you not believe it? I am sorry to smash down the walls of your ivory tower, but I have to break it to you that it is the kind of thing that happens all the time and, from the way you have described his domestic surroundings, I should judge Oliver to be more vulnerable than most.'

'Oh, I'm not denying that. It was his reaction which didn't ring true. For instance, when I asked him how this mugger could have known so accurately which house the keys belonged to, he was completely floored and he obviously hadn't given it a thought. Now, wouldn't you expect that to be one of the first things he'd start wondering about?'

'He'd had a nasty shock and was still feeling bemused, I daresay.'

'He wasn't hurt and he'd had the whole night to recover. I don't see why his brain shouldn't have been functioning normally by then. And it wasn't only that he hadn't given any thought to it himself, but when I brought it to his attention that Mugs might have been someone who recognised him, he just slid away from the subject and let it die, which I call most unnatural.'

'And, understanding as I do the devious workings of your so-called mind, I daresay you have now convinced yourself that either Mugs didn't exist, or was someone well known to Oliver, but whose identity he has some secret and probably shameful reason for wishing to conceal. In other words, he too is up to something?'

'You're right, both explanations had occurred to me, and

99

not without justification, in my opinion. For example, how do you account for his tearing round to our house, when he had so many urgent matters to deal with, in order to spend ten minutes with Philip? Quite unnecessary, one would have thought; and another point I'd like to draw your attention to is his strange reluctance to call the police. I could understand that attitude when the play was teetering on the edge of disaster and he was anxious to avoid a single whiff of bad publicity to tip it right over; but that's all finished now and the reluctance remains as strong as ever. I mean, tell me, honestly, Toby, wouldn't you have expected the first move on getting home after being mugged would be to dial 999? The man couldn't have got far away in those three or four minutes and if they'd been able to nab him before he ditched the credit cards they'd have been home and dry. Yet, according to Clarrie, he did nothing of the sort, just sat around moaning about getting the locks changed. I find it inexplicable.'

'Then let me explain! I realise that your faith in our wonderful police is such as to move mountains, which is as it should be, but most people regard it as a shocking waste of time to spend half an hour answering questions, only to be told that there is no reason to hope that anything can be done about it. What I find slightly more inexplicable is that he did not fly to the telephone and get the credit cards cancelled. That would be my first move, if I were ever unfortunate enough to be in his position.'

'Yes, I hadn't thought of that. You have added one more puzzle to the list and here comes the last one, which in my view beats the lot. Apart from taking no action after the mugging, are you aware that neither did he bother to report the burglary? You'd have thought he'd have done that to satisfy the insurance company, if nothing else.'

'And, in fact, I distinctly remember your telling me that he had done so and the police were on their way?'

'That's what he said, yes; about twenty minutes before Mr

Barksfield and I arrived. I believed him at the time, but not any more.'

'Why ever not?'

'Because I was there for another fifteen or twenty minutes, making a total of half an hour and there still wasn't a copper in sight. Oliver passed this off very airily by saying that no-one could ever find the place and he often had to wait in for a whole morning for someone to come and do a repair job, but that won't do for the local branch, will it? Even supposing they didn't know the whereabouts of every nook and cranny in the area, they have things called maps, you know, and it's my belief that Oliver had neither rung them up, nor had any intention of doing so.'

'I wonder why not?'

'As I keep repeating, it can only be for one of two reasons. Either the mugging and the burglary didn't happen, or else they did and he knows who the culprit was and prefers to keep it to himself.'

'And which strikes you as the more likely?'

'Couldn't hazard a guess, but there's one thing I am sure of.'

'Oh, good! What's that?'

'Whatever the answer, I'm willing to bet it's tied up in some way with those anonymous letters.'

CHAPTER TWELVE

I

The sevice was better attended than I had expected, almost a full house, in fact, although, conceivably, more than half the congregation had been drawn there by curiosity, rather than affection for the deceased. If so, they probably felt that it had been worth the trouble because Philip, so often a better actor off stage than on, gave a plucky performance. He had dug out a wide-brimmed, black homburg hat, which certainly made him conspicuous and he got his timing right too. By making some trivial excuse to return to the house when we had got as far as the gate, he contrived to hold up the action by arriving several minutes late and pausing inside the church for at least one more after removing the hat. Then, leaning heavily on my arm, the very picture of dignified grief, he embarked at last on his slow progress up the aisle to the front pew.

Our departure was made in similar style and evidently had such an awesome effect on all present that only a handful of people had the temerity to shuffle up and mutter a word or two of condolence. These included the Vicar and family solicitor, although not Anthony Blewiston, whom I had noticed sitting on his own near the back of the church when we went in, but who had vanished by the time we came out again.

We had agreed in advance that in the circumstances it would be both unnecessary and inappropriate to invite anyone back to the house for sherry and biscuits, but Philip and I were both in need of something more reviving than those and we covered the short distance back to The Old Rectory at twice the speed with which we had left it. I was relieved to

102

discover that the well-drilled Mrs Gale had been far-sighted enough to leave a tray bearing glasses, ice and assorted bottles on a table in the drawing room.

As soon as Philip had been relieved of his hat and installed in an armchair, with a gin and tonic in his hand, I told him that I would leave him for a few minutes to go and clean up and, when I came downstairs again, I turned left instead of right and made for the morning room. I had only the smallest hope of finding the newspapers still in the drawer where I had last seen them, but nevertheless considered it would be remiss and perhaps a touch cowardly not to grab this opportunity to try my luck. The fact that the door was not completely shut seemed to endorse this decision, since it enabled me to push it wide open and enter the room without making a sound.

Having done so, the only reward I got for my pains was a shock of major proportions. Philip was seated in the desk chair, which he had swivelled round to face the door. There was a long, thick white envelope across his knees, but he was not looking at it. His expression said plainer than words that he had been waiting for me.

'Looking for something?' he asked pleasantly.

'Well, no, that is, only the telephone. I wanted to ring up Toby and let him know what time I'd be back. I knew you wouldn't mind.'

'My dear girl, why should I mind. Ring up anyone you please. It's all right, if I stay, I suppose? Nothing private?'

'No, of course not.'

'Good, because when you've said what you have to say to him I have something to show you. It's Dolly's will. I thought you might be interested, you and I being such old and trusted friends. More like father and daughter, I often say.'

Toby has a phobia about the telephone and rarely picks it up, if Mrs Parkes, the housekeeper, is there to do it for him, which this time, to my relief, she was. It provided a reprieve of sorts and an extra minute or two while she fetched him to dredge up some slightly more pressing reason for calling him, since I was aware that the news about the time of my return was liable to be greeted by loud expressions of total indifference. I had worried unnecessarily, however, for he began by saying: 'Thank God you've rung up at last! What time will you be back?'

'Well, pretty soon, actually. That's really what I wanted to tell you. I mean Philip's borne up tremendously well and I don't think he needs me here much longer.'

'Oh, the hell with him! I'm the one who needs extricating.'

'Why? What have you got mixed up in?'

'A persecution. That boring friend of yours never stops badgering me. She's been at it for a couple of hours now.'

'Which friend? Clarrie?'

'Who else? The latest threat, as relayed to me by Mrs Parkes, is to come over and squat here until you return, so make it as quick as you can.'

'What's she in a state about now, do you know?'

'No, and I don't care. If you can head her off, please do so. It's all I ask.'

'Okay, I'll do my best, but it may mean that I shan't be back as early as I had expected.'

His reply to this was unrepeatable and I could only trust it was not spoken loud enough for Philip to overhear.

Ten minutes later and still in the morning room, I said to my trusted friend and father-resembler: 'You'll contest it, of course?'

'I don't know. It was what I was going to ask you. What do you advise?'

'I can't tell you what your chances would be, Philip, if that's what you mean. What does your solicitor say?'

'He's not my solicitor, he's Dolly's. That's to say, he acted for us both, but she was the one who handled all our legal affairs and, up to now, there's never been any conflict of interests. He didn't come right out with it, but I had the impression that he wouldn't be particularly keen to support me in getting the will revoked, if that's what they call it.'

'Understandable, I suppose, if he was the one who drew it up. You'll have to find someone else to take it on.'

'A complete stranger? I don't care for that idea at all. And it's not going to look very good, is it?'

'What isn't?'

'Oh, all those reporters hounding me . . . gossip writers making a meal of it. Rather hard at my age, you know,' he added in a tearful voice.

'Hard enough at any age, but people have had to do worse things than that for money and, anyway, all that side of it will very quickly die down and be forgotten.'

'Oh, easy for you to say that, Tessa! You've got your whole life ahead of you. It's different when you're old and tired like me and only have a few years left.'

'Then you'd better let me start by asking Robin whether he considers the game would be worth the candle. He's not an expert, but he knows a bit more about the law than we do and his advice is usually sound.'

'Oh, do what you like about it, it's entirely up to you,' Philip said, speaking as though he was the one who was conferring a favour, which, to be fair, in a sense perhaps he was.

II

It was the hollow-eyed, Greek tragedy Clarrie who greeted me a couple of hours later.

'I know I look terrible,' she announced, in case I hadn't noticed it, 'but I haven't closed my eyes since I last saw you and I do think you might have stirred yourself to get here a bit sooner.'

'I know and I'm sorry, but I had some business to finish off with Philip and I stopped on the way for a sandwich. I thought I'd be in a more constructive mood after some lunch and I had a feeling your cupboard might be bare.'

'You were so right. I couldn't even think of food in this crisis.'

'So what's it all about?'

'I'd better let Pete tell you himself. Come on in!'

'Oh, so Pete's back in favour, is he?' I asked, following her on to the verandah. 'Honestly, Clarrie, I find it hard to keep pace.'

He was not only back, but quite at home again, lying stretched out on the li-lo on his stomach, reading a magazine. He rolled over when we came in, swung his legs sideways on to the floor and sat up, all in one graceful movement.

'He's in very deep trouble,' Clarrie said, disregarding her own advice, 'and you've got to help pull him out of it. It's about that silly trick he played of going round to her lady-ship's flat on the night she was killed.'

'Care for a drink, Tessa?'

'No thanks, Pete, just had lunch. So it was you?'

'Of course it was him, don't be stupid! And I could really throttle him for being so idiotic. The trouble is that noblesse oblige won't allow me to because it was all for my sake. Chivalry running riot!'

'So far, it sounds like good news to me. No-one has much doubt it was him the lady saw and that the story about going back to the shop to collect your present was all my eye. If he can now produce some credible reason for being at the flat, it might not get him removed from the suspect list, but it could help.'

'If only you two harpies would stop talking about me as though I wasn't here! And the question is, my dear Tessa, will they find the reason credible, or won't they? Clarrie, who is on my side, took a bit of convincing, which is not what you'd call a hopeful sign.'

'Then why not try it out to me?'

'Why else do you think we wanted you here, you fool?' Clarrie asked. 'My idea, as it happens. Little Don Quixote here was against it, but I explained to him that you understood workings of the law and order mentality rather better than we do and we might as well use you as a guinea pig. It's all mixed up with those bloody boring old anonymous letters.'

'You don't say? Did Pete write them?'

'No, he thought perhaps I had.'

'That is not true, Clarrie, I never said that. What I said was that I was afraid some people with nasty minds, in which category I include the police, might think you had.'

'It amounts to the same thing.'

'No, it does not. Where are you going, Tessa?'

'Home,' I replied. 'You'll have to find someone else to be your guinea pig. I've had a tiring day, I only have an hour or two before I have to drive back to London and I have no intention of spending them listening to you two bickering.'

Luckily for me, it worked and Pete said: 'Yes, sorry, Tessa! How would it be if you were to exercise some superhuman self-control and keep your beautiful trap shut for about five minutes, Clarrie, while I tell her my own way? How clearly do you remember the wording on those letters?'

'Clearly enough.'

'Then you'll recall that the first two had what one might call a religious theme?'

'Which is why you thought they might have been inspired by Clarrie?'

'No, I did not. You're as bad as she is. That's the last sort of trick I'd associate with our Clarrie. If she had a grudge against someone enough to want to kill them, which she nearly always has, she'd have been shouting the news at the top of her lungs all over London.'

'I agree and, furthermore, the religious theme was dropped after the first two letters, so where's the problem?'

'Right there, in the fact that it was dropped. By that time several kind people had commented on the fact that Clarrie was the only one of our lot who was up on scripture, so if she had written them she'd have realised her mistake at that point and switched to a new line. At least, it seemed to me, that's what people would think. You with me?'

'I think so. Did Dolly tell you she'd given Oliver an ultimatum? Either he'd go to the police with the letters, or she'd do so herself?'

'Yes, you have caught up. She not only told me, but I knew she meant every word of it. She also told me she'd refused to hand over the letters to him because she had a shrewd idea that it would be as good as throwing them on the fire.'

'Which is when you decided to act?'

'Yes, and not only for Clarrie's sake, mark you, although that did come into it, but I thought it would be a hell of a lark to snatch the letters and then, when the grand moment of truth arrived, after all her squawks and threats, there she'd be with egg on her face.'

'Did she tell you where she'd hidden them?'

'Good as. She said she'd locked them away in a safe place, which was a first-class give-away. I could just visualise that potty little wall safe in her bedroom and the sort of picture that'd be covering it. A print, most likely, about twelve by ten, in a very light frame, so that it wouldn't be too much of a chore taking it down and putting it back again.'

'How come you know so much about the middle-class, older, rich woman's psychology?' Clarrie asked, breaking out of her heroic restraint at last.

'Oh well, one comes up against a funny lot in my line of business, you know. Believe it or not, I was once on friendly terms with a professional burglar, until he ran into a patch of bad luck and retired from public life. Fascinating chap and a great raconteur. I picked up quite a few tips from him about safe-breaking and so on.'

'Which eventually came in useful?' I suggested. 'Very daring of you, as an amateur, to put the advice into practice.'

'No, not all that. I knew the coast would be clear and I'd have all the time I needed to work in, but I put it off till nine o'clock because I thought there'd be less chance then of running into any of the other tenants. It didn't work out like that, though, as you probably know, and it was bad luck that nosey bitch turning up just when she did. I wished then I'd taken the trouble to make myself up a bit, wear a hat at least, but I'd reckoned on most people either being safe indoors by that time, or else out for the whole evening. Still, I wasn't all that bothered. Even if it came out that someone looking a bit like me had called there, I didn't think it was likely her ladyship would bother to let the police know that she was short of a few scraps of brown paper.'

'But it was much worse than that, of course?'

'Yes. When I walked in and saw her flopped over like that, purple in the face and dead as a doornail I nearly screamed. I had a job to stop myself rushing straight out into the corridor again. But I knew I had to keep my head, see? There was always the chance that Mrs Nosey wouldn't have given up and, if she was on the watch and saw me come bursting out, hell bent for the lift, I could be in dead trouble. So I stuck it out for three or four minutes and I was thankful I had. The blasted woman had left her door open and I knew damn well she was watching every move.'

'So there you have it, Tessa, and what Pete and I want to know from you is whether he should confess all, or leave things as they are. He and I are not in agreement over it, so you must decide.'

'Clarrie's for and I'm against and you want to know why? You can bet your life they'd manage to twist it around in some way to tighten the noose. I gather from what they tell me that you'd be on her side.'

'Yes, I was until I learnt that your little adventure was connected with the anonymous letters. Now I'm inclined to move over to yours.'

'What difference do they make?'

'Oh, all the difference, I'm afraid.'

'Explain!'

'Well, can't you see, Pete, that when you repeat what Dolly had told you about her hiding place and how, as a result, you'd guessed the letters would be hidden in a wall safe in her bedroom, they'll regard it as very astute thinking and that's where you run into your first snag.'

'Why?'

'You didn't, by any chance, spend those three or four minutes verifying your guess and rifling the safe?'

'Hell, no. It could have taken anything up to half an hour and anyway the idea never entered my head. All I could think of was ducking out of there at the first moment it'd be safe to show my face outside.'

'So there's your answer!'

'I still don't get it.'

'The police will want to know why it was that when they carried out their own search only a couple of hours later there were no papers of that kind, either in the safe or anywhere else. Also why no-one has made one single reference to them and there is no evidence to prove they ever existed.'

'Now I know you're barmy,' Clarrie said in a disgusted voice. 'Dozens of people can swear with their hands on their hearts that they existed. I'm one of them and you're another. Obviously, what happened was that someone must have got there before Pete, ran slap into her ladyship, who wasn't in the mood to take the intrusion lying down, finished her off and then started on the safe.'

'Yes,' I agreed, 'there's an outside chance that's how it was, but it's stretching it a bit, wouldn't you say?'

110

'Not at all, it's bloody staring you in the face.'

'So long as you find it credible that two separate people called at the flat within hours of each other and for exactly the same purpose. It would take a bit of swallowing.'

'The fact remains that it could have happened, but if it amuses you just to pick holes in everything, go ahead and enjoy yourself.'

'It's not for my own enjoyment, I'm just warning you what the official reaction is likely to be. Judging by his thoughtful expression, I imagine Pete agrees with me. It may have dawned on him by now that these two separate visitors had yet another thing in common.'

'What's that? What's she on about now, Pete?'

He did not reply and I did so for him: 'You may not know this, either of you, but the safe wasn't damaged in any way. It hadn't been forced open, which means that what we're faced with now is that whoever got there ahead of Pete either was or had been a professional burglar, or had become very chummy with one at some period of his life and had picked up some useful tips about safe-breaking.'

'Or it could have been opened with a key,' Clarrie said. 'Why not?'

'Why not indeed, except that that would also need a certain degree of expertise in burglary,' I reminded her, throwing everything I'd got into my meaning look at Pete. 'You don't just walk up to someone and say "I wonder if I might borrow the key of your safe for an hour or two?" So, whichever way you look at it, there's a lot of coincidence about and I'm afraid there are some nasty minds who are going to come up with the idea that he invented the story, and what a noble, unselfish one at that, as an excuse for having been caught letting himself into the Mickletons' flat that evening.'

'But it was true, you know, every word of it. It was all for my sake, or nearly all anyway. Isn't that so, Pete? Besides, how could anyone say he made it up when dozens of people will be able to say the silly old letters did exist and will also be able to remember what they said?'

'The trouble is that his story differs from everyone else's, in that he claims Dolly had told him in such detail where the letters were hidden. Very likely she did, but my guess is that the only other people she confided in to this extent were Philip and Oliver, and I am sorry to report that they both appear to have some good reason for denying that she told them anything of the kind.'

'Why would they deny it?'

'I don't know, but the fact is that neither of them has seen fit to mention it, so far, which I take to be a bad sign and I have a nasty suspicion that, if they were questioned about it, you would find them both saying that, to the best of their knowledge, the letters had been destroyed before Dolly was killed.'

'So that's that then, and a fat lot of good you've been! Now what are we going to do, I'd like you to tell me!'

'Why do you have to do anything?' I asked, as she walked out to the car with me. 'I can't see why knowing about it has made you any worse off than you were before. Pete hasn't been arrested and isn't likely to be, so long as they don't turn up any fresh evidence against him, so what are you agitating about?'

'You don't know the half of it!'

'Okay, tell me the other three quarters.'

'He's obsessed with the idea that they've got it in for him. I don't quite understand why, to be honest. There was some brush he had with them years ago over a drunk-driving charge which he swears they rigged, and it seems to have left some indelible scars. I don't know all the details, but nothing will shake him out of the idea that they're going all out to dig up something disreputable against him and, if they don't find it, they'll invent it.'

112

'No, they won't. That's nonsense!'

'Try telling him that! He says, once they've got some tiny mark against you, you don't stand a chance when something like this ghastly murder turns up. That's why he walked out on me last Sunday. It was getting him down, being on his own here all Saturday evening, when I was at that rotten boring party, that he couldn't sleep for thinking about it. So he got up early and spent the whole day mooning around the countryside.'

'But it's only this silly prejudice that makes him feel victimised, isn't it? All in the mind, as they say?'

'I don't know, Tessa, I honestly don't but it's going to drive us both out of them, if it doesn't stop soon. He says now that both our telephone lines are being tapped. I can't say I've noticed anything funny about them, but maybe he's right and that's not much fun, is it?'

'They can tap away till kingdom come, but it won't make any difference, so long as he has nothing to hide.'

'Of course, he hasn't anything to hide. Everything he told you about going to the flat and finding her ladyship dead was the stark, naked truth. He doesn't know any more than anyone else who got there first.'

I did not dispute this, since my reservations arose from the fact that he had not, by a very long chalk, been honest with her about his youthful tangle with the police and that therefore his current activities in the antique business might also be open to question.

Nor did I consider it advisable to precipitate another row between them by suggesting that she might ask him whether all the driving around during the weekend had been quite so aimless and blameless as he would have her believe.

CHAPTER THIRTEEN

I

'So who does get the money?' Robin asked towards the end of dinner.

'The stepdaughter in South Africa, who hasn't even bothered to put in an appearance. Isn't that incredible? Dolly had scarcely set eyes on her after the father died. Apparently the Mickletons sponged on her for free board and lodging during the South Africa tour the year before last and, when she came over last summer, she returned the compliment by spending a couple of weekends at The Old Rectory, but apart from that there hardly seems to have been any communication at all.'

'Although I suppose you could argue that, as the money had come from her father, in the first place, giving it back was a matter of conscience?'

'According to Philip, she was perfectly well provided for. Lashings of money around, by the sound of it and, anyway, I doubt if Dolly had a conscience. Poor old Philip, I do hope he didn't kill her. Imagine going to all that trouble, only to find himself worse off than he was before!'

'Doesn't he get anything?'

'Only the house, which luckily was bought in his name. I suppose that'll fetch quite a packet, but it can't be a quarter of what he was expecting and he'll still have to find somewhere else to live.'

'So long as he doesn't get the idea that our spare room might do to be going on with! How's he taking it?'

'Surprisingly calmly, almost as though he'd been prepared

for it. The only thing that really seemed to worry him was how it was going to look in the *News of the World*.

'Which at least puts paid to any suggestion that he was the one who went to the trouble of murdering her?'

'Yes, I suppose so.'

'Well, doesn't it?'

'I'm sure that it does. Philip may not have the sharpest brain in the world, but even he would have the wits to see that to collapse into transports of shock/horror would strike the wrong note. He would at least know enough to put on an act of being resigned.'

'But the point is, surely, that it doesn't need to be an act. You say that he appeared to have been expecting it and I should think the chances are that he was. It's quite normal for married couples to discuss their wills and presumably Philip knew all about the terms of hers. It didn't bother him because neither of them expected for one minute that he would out-live her.'

'I don't see why she wouldn't have taken such a contin-gency into account. People of all ages can get killed in motor accidents or drop dead from heart attacks. It doesn't have to be anything as way out as murder and that argument would apply particularly to Dolly, if she was the hypochondriac Philip makes her out to be.'

'Not necessarily. Hypochondriacs don't really believe they're going to die in the foreseeable future, any more than anyone else. I sometimes think they believe it less than anyone else. And, anyway, if Philip wasn't prepared for it, again why bother to put on an act? A degree of surprise and disappoint-ment would be only natural in the circumstances. There would be nothing incriminating about it.'

'Yes, I agree with you.'

'You do? So what are we arguing about?'

'I see it all clearly now and it is you who have opened my eyes. He probably was putting on an act, but, being such an incurable ham, he overdid it. He was so anxious not to betray the shock/horror that he went to the other extreme and pretended to be indifferent.'

'I can't quite fathom whether, in your view, that confirms his guilt or his innonence, but no doubt you have taken your theory a stage or two further?'

'No, I haven't and I don't intend to. I admit to feeling curious about who killed her, but no more than that. She was not a nice woman and I have no great urge to see her murderer brought to justic. I shall leave that to the professionals. Are they making any headway, incidentally?'

'Not so's you'd notice, I gather. It's proving a tough one to crack. They've interviewed countless people in and around the apartment block, but it hasn't brought any results. There's no porter, you see, only that caretaker type in the basement and, except in cases of emergency, he's off duty by five thirty; something which the murderer was doubtless aware of. The only conclusion left is that it must have been someone she knew and trusted, but that still leaves a pretty wide field and there's no way of telling what device he used to get into the flat.'

'What are the options?'

'Did they meet outside and go there together? Did he ring the outside bell and announce himself, either with his own name or a false one? Or was he someone who was in a position to get his hands on both keys and have duplicates made?'

'Like Pete?'

'Like Pete, and the chief trouble with him is, apart from not appearing to possess one glimmer of a motive, reputed in fact to have been on rather more amiable terms with the victim than most, he has an almost impeccable alibi.'

'Only almost?'

'It seems that no-one has a cast-iron, gold-plated impeccable one, with the possible exception of Oliver Welles.'

'What's so special about Oliver?'

116

Robin had taken a page from a memo pad out of his pocket and began to read aloud from it: "Five thirty-eight p.m. Deposited his car in an underground car park two hundred yards north of Shaftesbury Avenue. Regular customer, known to staff, time confirmed. Six twenty. Seen entering theatre by stage door keeper, who spoke to him." He stopped and then added:

'Not conclusive, I grant you, but it allows him approximately forty minutes, which he claims to have spent eating a sandwich at a pub on his way down to the theatre, to get to the Mickletons' flat, make his way inside, commit the murder and return to base. Not really long enough, seeing that on the outward journey he'd have been travelling with the rush-hour traffic and therefore slowed down almost to walking pace part of the time; whereas coming back he'd have been caught up in the beginnings of the surge towards the West End theatres and movies. He might, with exceptional luck, have found a cruising taxi for each trip, but it would still have been very tight.'

'Yes, it would. Any witnesses at the pub?'

'As it happens, no, but that's not as damning as it sounds. All those places in Soho are crammed to the lid at that hour; people meeting each other at the start of the evening, or dashing in for a quick one on their way home. He has the reputation of scarcely setting foot inside a pub as a rule and he said he'd never been in this one before in his life, so it's not so surprising that none of the staff remembers seeing him on that occasion or any other. However, it's the time element which counts most in his favour. They've tested it with three separate experiments and the one which came closest to equalling it over-ran by twelve minutes.'

'How about the others?'

'Well, as you know, it was established that death had occurred between five thirty and six thirty, allowing for a few minutes either way, which is the worst possible time for alibi checking. It is just the period when most people are on their way home from work, or, in this case, on their way to it and that gives scope for endless manipulation. It's easy enough, as a rule, to pin down to within minutes what time someone left one place and arrived at the next, but he can say he walked the whole way and that it took him forty minutes; that he waited half an hour at a bus stop, or that he crawled along in his car at three miles an hour through the rush-hour traffic. All these claims are just as likely to be true as false, so you may not be surprised to hear how many people have trotted them out.'

'No, I'm not, but to go back to what you were saying before, Robin, about what trick the murderer used to get into the flat; if I were sticking my oar in, which as you know I'm not, it would be the last one you mentioned which would receive most attention from me.'

'That he'd got hold of the keys? Why do you see that as the most likely?'

'Because, if Philip is right in believing she was scared of something like this happening and wrote the letters herself, either to get police protection or in the hope of its acting as a deterrent to her would-be murderer, then it's hard to imagine her taking someone back to the flat with her at a time when she knew they would be alone there. It's less likely still, in my opinion, that she would have released the catch on the main door, if he'd rung her bell.'

'You may be right, but you have to remember, you see, that the people in charge of the case have never heard of those anonymous letters. Which reminds me to tell you it's one thing not to stick your oar in and, in general, I'm all for it, but it's quite another to go round advising people to suppress evidence.'

'What evidence? A drawerful of newspapers and brown paper wouldn't provide much to work on, specially as there doesn't seem to be a single example left of the finished product. And, if there were, it still wouldn't give any clue to the murderer's identity, if we accept that she wrote them herself.'

'It could still be helpful to know that she believed someone was trying to kill her.'

'Well, that's for Philip to tell them. I have no first-hand knowledge of it, so it's not for me to interfere. And he wouldn't be much use either, since he insists that she never mentioned it to him, far less that he has any idea who she could have been afraid of.'

'And don't you find that faintly incredible? Her not mentioning it, I mean?'

'No, not particularly. She would have gone to any lengths, rather than allow him to be worried or upset, with this crucial first night almost upon them. It was an obsession with her, her mission in life, you might say. I'm told it had got to the point where she took it on herself to open all his letters, in case one of them contained bad news or a nasty bill. The only way he managed to escape from her eternal vigilance was to go and spend an hour or two at his club. They don't allow women in there.'

'I wonder she didn't force him to resign.'

'She probably would have, if she hadn't been such an arrant snob, but it happens to be a club which numbers a great many celebrated actors and writers among its members, so that was the one bolthole which hadn't been put out of bounds.'

'And I am sorry to tell you that you have spent the last three minutes flatly contradicting yourself.'

'Really? How have I managed to do that?'

'If, as you maintain, her principal object was to spare him worry and anxiety, don't you find it paradoxical that she should have sent the letters to herself? If anything was designed to bring on an attack of worry and anxiety, one would have said that was it.'

'Yes, it does seem incongruous, on the face of it.'

'Putting it mildly!'.

'I didn't exactly overlook the point, though, Robin. At

119

first, like you, I took the view that it made nonsense of Philip's theory, but now I'm not so sure. After all, if she believed herself to be in great peril, it would have called for desperate measures and let's assume that she sent the first letter as an experiment. If it had knocked Philip out and struck terror into his heart, she'd most likely have dropped it like a hot potato and tried some other dodge. It would have been just a one-off affair, leading nowhere and soon forgotten; and Philip would have had three clear days to recover and calm down before the opening night. But, as you know, that wasn't how it worked out. He was the least concerned of anyone, maybe a little too unconcerned for her liking, but at least it left her free to continue her campaign, to the point where she could blackmail, or rather con, Oliver into calling in the police, which is what she had been aiming for all along.'

As I finished speaking, the front door bell rang and we both instinctively glanced up at the grandfather clock, which responded politely by starting to strike ten. Between the eighth and ninth chimes the bell rang again and Robin got up from the table and left the room.

'Do be careful!' I called after him, but he did not bother to reply and I daresay there was no need. Whatever his faults, carelessness is not one of them.

II

Two minutes later he was back, preceded by Oliver, looking as bleached as one of his own handkerchiefs and tumbling over himself with apologies: 'Do forgive me, Tessa! I know this is unpardonable, but something rather tricky has come up, which you might be able to help me with. Oh, I see you're still at dinner! How awful of me!'

'That's all right, we've finished now. What's the trouble? Something to do with the play?'

'Well, yes, indirectly, I suppose you could say that.'

'That being so', Robin told him, 'I'll leave you to it. You won't need me and I have some work to catch up with before I go to bed.'

Taking this to be a euphemism for stacking up the dishwasher, I did not try to detain him.

'Do sit down, Oliver. Would you like some coffee? It's still fairly hot.'

'Oh no, thank you very much. It keeps me awake and that's one thing I don't need at the moment.'

'Well, I can't imagine what help I could be, but I suppose what you really need is a shoulder to cry on?'

'Not exactly. The fact is, I was hoping for some practical advice.'

'On what?'

'It's a long story, but I'll be as brief as I can. You remember the night of my party?'

'When you were mugged?'

'Exactly! I have to confess that there was more to that story than I told you.'

'You didn't make it up, by any chance?'

'Make it up? What an extraordinary suggestion! No, I did not.'

'And you still have no idea who the man was?'

'None, and that's what I find so disturbing.'

'Because you realise it must have been someone you know?'

'That's one reason. It hadn't occurred to me until you pointed it out, but then I saw that you must be right. That threw me a bit, but the real worry is a little matter of some keys.'

'But surely, now that you've had the locks changed . . . Oh well, we'll be at it all night, if I keep interrupting you. Go on!'

Oliver paused, took a deep breath, then pulled out his handkerchief and gave his glasses a rub up: 'I feel ashamed of myself in confessing this, Tessa, but the truth is, I'm not referring to my own keys, this was another set. They belong to the Mickletons' flat.'

'Do they indeed? So what were they doing in your pocket and how long had they been there?'

'Since almost a week ago. Last Wednesday to be precise.'

'My God, Oliver, that was the day when . . .'

'When Dolly was murdered? Yes, I'm afraid it was, but you needn't look at me like that. I didn't kill her, I assure you. I didn't even use the keys. I had intended to, but I didn't.'

'But how : . . Oh, wait a minute, I believe I've got it now! They were the keys Philip thought he'd left at home when we took him back that evening? He hadn't done anything of the kind, you'd nicked them?'

'Not so. I borrowed them, and with every intention of returning them, only the opportunity never arose.'

'But what did you borrow them for?'

'To get my hands on the letters. On Wednesday morning Dolly marched into my office and fairly let fly. Bullying and threatening and carrying on like the Gestapo. What it boiled down to was an ultimatum. Either I would inform the police about Anon within the next twenty-four hours, or she would do so herself. I tried not to show it, but I was so angry I could hardly speak. What right had she to come strutting in and order me about? You had already warned me what would result from the police getting involved and how could I allow that to happen at such a moment? It seemed so totally unnecessary and unfair too, since Philip didn't appear to be in the least bothered.'

'So what did you say to her?'

'That I would think it over; and as soon as she left I went along to the theatre to have a chat with Philip. I had calmed down a bit by then and I saw that my only hope was to try and persuade him to use his influence to postpone matters until after the first night. I knew I could probably catch him on his own, for once, because Dolly had told me in her gracious way that she was only prepared to spare me five minutes, as she was on her way to an important committee meeting.'

'And how did he react?'

'I never saw him. There was a photograph call when I arrived, so I went up to his room to wait for him. His dresser wasn't there either. I was just about to sit down when I noticed a pile of odds and ends on his shelf. There was a cheque book among them, I remember, one or two letters and the keys. I acted on impulse.'

'Grabbed the keys and ran?'

'It's so hard to explain. I had never in my life thought to do such a thing and my only excuse is that I do not think I can have been quite myself. I was sick with worry, about a number of things, quite unconnected with Dolly and those wretched letters and I had been sleeping badly. Also, I suppose, the rational side of me had always known that enlisting Philip's support had been something of a forlorn hope. He was always too weak and lazy to stand up to her.'

'So you settled for a little breaking and entering instead?'

'I'd been to their flat before, you see, several times, when we were drawing up Philip's contract. So I knew the drill and I timed it all very carefully. Much good that did me! I appear to have no more talent for crime than for any other potentially profitable activity,' he added with a snort of laughter.

'Not many people have, I imagine, without the proper training and apprenticeship. What went wrong in your case?'

'It was the night of the preview, as you know. I put my car in the usual place, near the theatre and then stopped by at the stage door to find out if Philip was in. They told me he was and, in my innocence, it never entered my head that Dolly wouldn't be with him.'

'So off you sped to Mickleton Towers? What happened when you got there?'

'Still playing it cautious, which seems such a sour joke now, I got the cab driver to drop me off in a street round the corner from the flat and I walked the last fifty yards. I felt quite elated with myself for having taken that precaution, like a child pretending to be some television private eye character, though quite what purpose it was supposed to serve now escapes me.'

'Never mind, we all need our fantasies to get us through these tricky moments. What happened?'

'Nothing at all is the short answer. I lost my nerve. I stood outside the front door for two or three minutes, with the keys in my hand, trying to work up the courage to use them, but I couldn't bring myself to do it. In the end I just slunk away, feeling more humiliated than ever before in my life.'

'I think your instinct had told you right. After all, this must have been very close to the time when she was killed. The murderer might still have been on the premises and then you'd have been really up the creek. You didn't see anyone, I suppose?'

'See anyone?'

'Going in or out of the building?'

Noticing that he took time out to polish his glasses before denying it, I did not consider it worth while pursuing the subject and instead asked him what he had done with the keys.

'Nothing. That word is beginning to sum up the story of my life. I fully intended to replace them at once. There was still time for it when I got back to the theatre and I'd planned to go along to Philip's room and wish him luck. Once again, I'd got every move worked out in advance. I'd station myself just inside the room, with my back to a chair and drop the keys down into it while I was talking, but I never got the chance. Benjie grabbed me the minute I got in. We were running late, among other things, so it was no time to go galloping around, popping into people's dressing rooms for friendly chats. And then, of course, the heat became more intense as the evening wore on. It came to the point where I forgot all about the damn keys until I got home that night and found them still in my pocket. Which is where they remained until they passed into the hands of my mugging friend.'

'But, Oliver, that was on Wednesday and you weren't mugged until Saturday. Three whole days! What on earth possessed you to hang on to them for all that time?'

'I'm not sure that I can account for it, even to myself. I'd been tempted once or twice to throw them away, make a parcel of them and put them in the dustbin, but something always stopped me. Whether it was some superstitious idea that they might somehow be found and traced back to me, or whether simply that it went against the grain to treat someone else's property in that way, I can't tell. I suppose I just told myself that sooner or later there'd be a chance to put them back where they belonged. I couldn't have foreseen where it would lead to, could I?'

'And at least one puzzle is now solved.'

'What puzzle?'

'I understand now why you didn't alert the police when you were mugged. And, of course, not having reported that incident would have prevented your giving an accurate account of the burglary as well. To put it plainly, you were afraid that, if by some unfortunate fluke they were able to catch the man and return your property, it just might lead to some embarrassing questions about Philip's keys.'

'Not a lot gets past you, does it, Tessa? I had no idea you had seen through my small evasion.'

'Oh well, I fancy myself at being able to tell when people are lying, but it's nothing to be proud of. I'm afraid it's mainly because I do it so often myself that I can see it coming from a mile off. Anyway, that's a comparatively minor point. The big mystery still remains.'

'I am not sure if I understand you.'

'Oh, come on, Oliver! You must have foreseen that I'd be wondering why you are telling me all this now? If not at the beginning, why is it necessary to take me into your confidence at all? Why, after two days has it become imperative to unburden yourself, so that you have to come tearing round here at ten o'clock at night?'

'It was the first chance I had. I telephoned this morning and they told me you'd be home for dinner.'

'And what had happened by the time you telephoned which made it so urgent that it couldn't wait until tomorrow?'

'The post had arrived.'

'Oh yes? And what did that bring?'

'A package containing all my own keys, including car keys.'

'But not Philip's?'

'Correct!'

'Very disturbing for you, I do see that. And no money or credit cards, not to mention the clock and other trifles he helped himself to while you were getting the Sunday papers?'

For the third time during this conversation Oliver removed his glasses, now staring down at them as though wondering who they belonged to, and I went on: 'Or did you, by any chance, invent that story of the burglary? Was it perhaps not true that when I arrived with Mr Barksfield the thief had just walked into the house and removed some of your possessions?'

'I am ashamed to admit that it was only half true.'

'Oh, I see! Well, how about telling me the other half?'

'He did use my keys to open the front door and let himself in. It is not true that anything was stolen.'

'But in that case, Oliver, how do you know he was there at all?'

'Because, although nothing was missing, several items had been returned, including the two you've just mentioned, and something extra had been added.'

'Something extra!'

'A sheet of writing paper, with a line of typing on it.'

'Saying what?'

'Saying: *Got You Where I Want You Now*. Nothing else, no signature.'

'Where was it?'

'In my typewriter. He'd taken the cover off and left the paper on the roller. I was appalled, literally shaking, with rage as well as shock. Then almost immediately I heard you coming, so I whipped the cover back on and tried to pull myself together enough to produce some plausible story to account for my state of nerves. I realised that I couldn't get away with the pretence that it was simply the after-effects of the mugging, specially since you'd brought the locksmith with you and, in theory, the worst of my troubles was over. So I invented a nice, neat burglary.'

'Have you kept the note?'

'No. When you'd gone, I nerved myself to go back for another look at it, half hoping, in the ridiculous way one does, that it wouldn't be there, that it was just a bad dream; but of course, it was there right enough. Sitting up on the typewriter and mocking me, just as he'd intended. It was the insolence of it which maddened me as much as anything. I scrumpled it up and threw it into the waste paper basket, trying to push it out of my mind, to force myself to believe that it had never existed. In any case, there would have been no point in keeping it, since he'd used my own writing paper and typed it on my own machine.'

'I wouldn't be too sure of that. Sometimes, if you study it long enough, even the most blatantly simple message can be found to contain more than first met the eye. And how about the package which arrived this morning? Any message with that?'

'No, nothing. A real cat and mouse game, isn't it? But I daresay the implication is clear enough. Blackmail would appear to be the name of this one. Presumably, the next communication will come over the telephone. It's getting to the point where I feel panicky about answering it. That's partly why I came out this evening. I knew, if it rang, that I'd have to pick it up and it was getting on my nerves, just sitting there and waiting for something to happen. Walking the streets was preferable to that.'

'So you didn't have it in mind to call here when you set out?'

'I suppose it must have been at the back of my mind, because I found myself walking in this direction. I can't really tell you why because I knew there wasn't more than a chance in a million of finding you alone.'

'So you wouldn't have told me, if Robin had been in the room?'

'Oh no, good heavens, no. I had my story prepared for that eventuality. I was going to ask you about Philip and how he had stood up to the funeral. Then I was going to drum up some excuse for not having gone to it. I ought to have been there, you see, and I did mean to go, I had every intention of it, but this thing in the post threw me completely and I couldn't face it. I had visions of sitting there in the church, knowing that this man could very easily be there too, perhaps in the very same pew, watching and gloating.'

'I doubt that. They seemed to be nearly all local people. The only one of our lot who bothered to turn up was Anthony, who always does the correct thing, and I can't see him playing a trick like this, can you? However, the important point is, Oliver, what will you do? What action do you propose to take? Or are you prepared just to sweat it out, shaking in your shoes every time the telephone rings, until the next bombshell lands in your lap?'

'What else can I do? I was hoping you might have some suggestion.'

'If this has been strictly for my ears alone, without even Robin to be told, I am afraid my advice would be unacceptable.'

'Meaning that you would recommend me to pass it over to the police? No, I couldn't do that. I've given it a lot of thought, but it would be too much of a gamble. The chances of being believed are so remote that I dare not risk it. At worst, I should be held on suspicion of murder; at best, they could do nothing more constructive than tell me to keep them informed of further developments. What use would that be?'

'So what is the alternative?'

'Sweat it out, as you say, and wait for the next move. I do feel somewhat calmer now that I've unburdened myself. It doesn't any longer loom quite so menacingly and I'm grateful to you for listening. I'll go now and leave you in peace, but I hope you'll bear with me if I keep you in the know with what follows?'

'Yes, do; and in the meantime I'll do some brain-racking on your behalf and hope for an inspiration.'

'That's really most kind!' he said, sounding as relieved and grateful as though he genuinely believed that his problems were now half-way to being solved.

CHAPTER FOURTEEN

Anthony Blewiston answered the telephone, throwing me off course and it flashed through my mind that I had dialled his number by mistake. However, as further reflection reminded me that I did not know Anthony's number, I asked him what he was doing there.

'Ministering to the sick. Who is that? Tessa?'

'Yes. Do you mean Philip? What's he sick of now?'

'Food poisoning, by the sound of it. He's in a bad way, poor fellow.'

'I'm sorry to hear that, but I still don't understand how you come to be there. I caught sight of you at the funeral, but then you vanished into the unknown.'

'Yes, I had an appointment to see a man about a pony. I was on my way home from there when it occurred to me that it would be the civil thing to pay a call on the bereaved. Just as well I get these charitable urges occasionally. This one turned into an overnight stop.'

'Good for you! How is he now?'

'Better. Still groggy though. He's had a rough time.'

'Has the doctor been?'

'Oh yes, I had to call him in. Couldn't take the responsibility, you know. Chap called Macintosh. Very nice man.'

'Yes, I know him of old. He's often in poor health himself and Toby's been diagnosing his ailments for years.'

'Well, he impressed me, I don't mind telling you. Left his dinner party to come speeding up here at nine o'clock and back again this morning, about half an hour ago. Pretty good service for nowadays.'

'And he said it was food poisoning?'

'Symptons indicated that. He was muttering about salmonella at one point, but he's thrown that idea out now.'

'Well, thank God for something, but what I don't understand is how he could have got it. He only had a few slices of ham and some salad for lunch. I know, because Mrs Gale put it out for him while I was there.'

'Ah well, there would appear to be a bit of a mystery there.'

'What could be mysterious about cold ham and salad?'

'It seems he took a whim to liven it up with a lump of pork pie which had been at the back of the refrigerator since who knows when. Probably had whiskers on it.'

'He must have been raving mad.'

'Yes, or perhaps he only imagined it. He was a bit delirious at one stage and apparently he didn't say a word about it to the doctor.'

'Too ashamed of himself, I should think. Can you stay tonight as well?'

'If I have to. Shan't know my fate for certain until Macintosh looks in again around tea time. I can't say I relish the prospect, but one can't exactly leave him here on his own, if he's not fit to look after himself and the mere mention of a nursing home throws him into a panic.'

'I know. It's a pity because a week or two in one of those would solve all our problems. Still, perhaps he couldn't afford it anyway. How about getting a nurse to come in for a few nights?'

'That was mooted too, but it seems they're also rather pricey and not easy to come by in these parts. He wasn't dead keen on that idea either.'

'I see. Well, listen, Anthony, will you call me again after the doctor's been and let me know the verdict? I have to go out now, but I'll be here this afternoon.'

'Whatever you say. Might you be able to come to the rescue?'

'If necessary, I suppose I could. The prospect doesn't please

me any more than it does you, but I feel responsible for the
old codger, in a way. Oh dear, how tiresome of Dolly to get
herself murdered without making proper provision for him!
She is turning out to be just as much of a trial now she is dead
as when she was alive.'

Soon after five he called me back.

'Good news, Tessa! No sacrifices from you will be needed.
Not for the present anyway.'

'You mean Philip's better?'

'Not noticeably, but other feet have stepped into the
breach.'

'Whose?'

'Oliver's. Isn't that something? He telephoned soon after I
spoke to you. Wanted to apologise to Philip for not turning
up at the funeral or something, and when I'd outlined the plot
he offered to come down this afternoon and stay for as long as
he was needed. How about that, eh?'

'Very noble!'

'Ah well, that's as maybe.'

'Why is it?'

'Not wishing to be snide, I had the impression he was
pretty keen to get out of London, for some reason. Don't
blame him for that, of course, but he's never struck me as the
country-loving type. I suggested he might as well hold his
horses until we'd had Dr Macintosh's report, but he said no,
he'd be down anyway. Funny sort of cove, isn't he?'

'I hope Philip is suitably grateful?'

'He was when he heard Oliver would be bringing his own
provisions. Dry goods, alcohol, the lot! Cheered him up no
end.'

'Sounds as though he's prepared for a siege.'

'Rather what I thought. I told him I didn't see the necessity
for that, seeing that he was the one who was putting himself
out, but he wouldn't have it. On the contrary, he said, he'd be

132

bringing some work down with him and it would be a good chance to get stuck into it, without incessant interruptions.'

'He has got it organised, hasn't he? Not proposing to install a couple of secretaries as well, by any chance?'

'You're not far off, believe it or not. He says, so long as Philip doesn't object, he'd like to have Benjie over during the daytime. No problem about finding a bed for him because his parents are only twenty miles away and he can stay with them. He's got it all worked out.'

'Except for one thing.'

'Oh? What's he overlooked?'

'It sounds to me as though he's got so carried away that he's lost sight of the original purpose. I doubt if Philip will have, though, and you don't need me to tell you that the incessant interruptions he can create will make Oliver's office seem like the Gobi desert by comparison.'

'You never spoke a truer word, old girl, but I don't think we should let it worry us. And, to be fair, he's not causing much mayhem at the moment. Bit drowsy most of the time.'

'Did the doctor give him a sedative?'

'Yes. Tried to, that is, but Philip wasn't having any of that nonsense. Said he's got cupboardfuls of sleeping pills in the house already and no need to go throwing money away on a fresh lot. Macintosh had a look at them and said they'd do, he'd prescribed them himself, in fact. So that's all in order and I should say we could leave him and Oliver to fight it out between them. I'm just waiting for him to get here, so I can show him the ropes and then full speed for home. If you take my advice, you'll stay out of it.'

Sound advice, too, in my opinion, although I was not able to heed it for long. The next pebble to ruffle the waters was thrown in by Oliver, who telephoned at ten o'clock the following morning and, with uncharacteristic terseness, asked me to go immediately to The Old Rectory.

'Philip's had another bad go during the night and he wants

133

to see you.'

'Have you called the doctor?'

'Yes, he came about an hour ago. Gave him something to stop the vomiting and it seems to be working.'

'So what am I supposed to do?'

'He won't say. All I know is that when I went in to see him just now he said he was feeling better, but it was urgent that I should get hold of you at once and tell you to come down. I asked him if there wasn't something I could do, which is, after all, what I'm supposed to be here for, but he said no, it had to be you and no-one else.'

'And you've no idea what it's about?'

'None.'

'Can't you put him on the line, so that he can tell me himself?'

'No, I suggested that too, but he says he doesn't feel strong enough and that anyway it's not a fit subject for discussion on the telephone. I hope you can manage to get here because I can see that I shan't have a minute's peace otherwise, and Benjie's due very soon. We were planning to get down to some figures.'

'Oh, very well, tell him I'll try and be there in a couple of hours. But where will it all end, I'm beginning to ask myself.'

CHAPTER FIFTEEN

I

It was Mrs Gale's morning for doing the weekly shopping and Oliver let me in. He had taken over the morning room and the desk was covered with ledgers and files. He offered me a drink from his private hoard and gave me the latest bulletin on Philip's health, which was now on the mend again.

'Where's Benjie?' I asked. 'Hasn't he come?'

'No, some family trouble, it appears. I was too bothered to find out the details, but his mother has been on the verge of a nervous breakdown for weeks, which is why he's had to spend so much time there recently. It's a damn nuisance, but not desperate. I can manage on my own, so long as I'm left in peace. It'll just take a little longer, that's all.'

'And time is not so important at present, is it? At least, while you are here, you feel safe from your persecutor?'

'Oh yes, there is that to be said for it and I must confess that my motives weren't entirely altruistic. It gave me the chance of a few days to simmer down and collect myself. Apart from you and Benjie, the only one who knows where I am is Anthony and, as you said, he hardly strikes one as a black-mailing type.'

'And you've heard no more from the real one?'

'Not a word. Of course, there may be something unpleasant waiting for me when I get back to London, but I am not so bothered now. If I were to be asked about the keys, I should simply say that they'd been left behind at the theatre after Philip collapsed and I thought it safer to take charge of them until he had recovered. It could never be proved that I'd

135

had them in my possession before the murder was committed, or that I'd used them. I can see things more objectively now.'

I considered it a curious way of putting it and was also struck by the transformation which only twenty-four hours of simmering down had brought about. Over-complacency now seemed to be the danger, but as it was not for me to dampen these soaring spirits, I said that I would leave him to get on with his work and go and pay some attention to Philip.

'Yes, all right, Tessa, and would you mind taking these letters up to him? He wasn't in a fit state to read them when the post arrived, but I see this one is marked urgent, so perhaps he ought to have it right away.'

'Hallo, Philip, how are you feeling?'

He was seated in an armchair by the window, wearing pyjamas and a dressing gown, but he did not look so feeble as I had expected, quite brisk, in fact. Two days of enforced sobriety had sharpened him up wonderfully, although it had not done anything for his temper.

'Ah, Tessa! So you've got here at last?'

'Yes, I've got here at last and I've brought you some letters.'

'Put them down on the bed. I'll deal with them later.'

'This one's from South Africa and it's marked urgent. Don't you think you ought to glance at it?'

'No, later, I said. First of all, there's something I want you to do for me. And sit down, for goodness sake! How can I talk to you when you keep hovering like that?'

I sat on the end of the bed and put the letters down beside me.

'That's better! Now, as I say, there's something I want you to do for me, but before I get to that, do you remember my telling you why I believed Dolly had made up those brown paper concoctions herself and with what object?'

'Certainly, I do. You also told me that she never gave you any hint that someone might want to kill her. Have you had second thoughts about that?'

'In a sense, I have, yes. Not because of anything she said. I wouldn't be likely to forget a thing like that, but naturally I've been giving it a good deal of thought since then; when I've felt well enough to think, that is.'

'And what has now struck you?'

'What has now struck me is that, if her object had been to ensure that the police were called in, wouldn't she have tried to provide some clue in the letters to make their job easier for them?'

'Such as?'

'Well, the wording, for instance?'

I pondered on this for a while, before saying: 'You refer to a well-known trick of Clarrie's, no doubt. But listen, Philip, various people have remarked on that already and . . .'

'Oh, use your wits, my dear child! Can't you see the difference between then and now? When those various people you mention were discussing it, they were under the impression that the letters had come from outside. Naturally, they agreed that, if Clarrie had sent them, she would have been much too sharp to have given herself away like that. The situation has altered now, because Dolly would have gone all out to introduce some hint about the identity of this enemy of hers and, for all her many wonderful qualities, it would be stupid to pretend that she was very perceptive about people. It's precisely the sort of trick she'd have used to draw attention to Clarrie and it was only when she found it wasn't working that she changed her tactics.'

'Yes, I've understood all that and it isn't what I was arguing about, because in effect what you're now saying is that Dolly believed Clarrie to be a murderess. I was about to remark that the aforementioned various people, who included myself, were all convinced that it was quite out of the question.'

137

'I don't happen to agree with you, but we can leave that aside because I'm not necessarily suggesting that she performed the deed herself. I consider it more likely that she put her young man up to it. You may find that equally inconceivable, but I don't. She happens to be one of the most sexually alluring young females that God ever put breath into, with quite extraordinary power over men. I can see him cheerfully killing off half the population of London, if that's what she wanted and I daresay, in my younger days, I'd have done the same.'

'Well, you're the authority on that subject, so I must take your word for it, but you still haven't explained what motive she could have had for wishing Dolly dead.'

'Ah, there, I must admit, you have me. Otherwise I shouldn't be wasting my time discussing it with you. I should already have passed it on to the Superintendent, make no mistake about that.'

'So I suppose you want me to pass it on to Robin instead, and ask him to see that it gets to the right quarter, without bringing your name into it?'

'No, nothing of the kind. How could I possibly expect my name not to be brought into it? And then what? I should have no evidence to bear me out, only my word that the letters existed and were phrased in that way, and I'd be back where I started. No, what I want you to ask Robin to do for me is to get this analysed.'

He had been groping in his dressing gown pocket while he spoke and now brought out a medicine bottle half filled with milky liquid. It was labelled with the name and address of a local chemist and underneath the handwritten words: *Lady Mickleton. 1-2 Tablespoons as required.*

'Is it poison?' I asked.

'That's what I want you to find out.'

'Seriously, Philip?'

'You remember my telling you about Dolly's imaginary

illnesses?'

I nodded and he went on.

'Like everyone who suffers in that way, she used to tear off to the doctor every time she sneezed and she was also fanatical about following his prescriptions to the letter. It hardly seemed to matter whether it was doing her any good or not, so long as she took the right dose at the right time. You get the picture?'

'Yes. I always thought all those pills and potions you had lying around were for your benefit, but I gather she was taking them herself?'

'Most of them, and the one you have there was the most recent addition to the collection. A few weeks before she died she had a bilious attack. I don't know what caused it and it didn't seem to be serious, but, as usual, she had Macintosh round here in a flash and this was what he prescribed. It was on a Saturday, I remember, and by Sunday evening she seemed to have got over it, but that wasn't enough for her. She insisted on taking what was left of the stuff up to London the next morning, so as to go on taking it until the bottle was empty.'

'But, obviously, she didn't?'

'No. A couple of days later she became really ill, sick as a dog for a whole night and that was when she picked up the idea that the medicine was causing it. She got some notion into her head that if she took it in combination with a certain kind of food, it would start up a chemical reaction, or some such tale, and she was furious with Macintosh for not having warned her. He wasn't too pleased about it, I may say. Good as told her she was talking rubbish, but he said that, so long as the stuff wasn't doing her any good, she might as well stop taking it and he'd give her something else.'

'And after that she was all right?'

'Far as I know. At any rate, she didn't refer to it again and, to tell you the truth, I'd forgotten all about it.'

'So why the sudden urge to get this analysed? No, on second thoughts, don't tell me because I've guessed. You've been taking it yourself?'

'That's it. I had this queasy turn soon after the funeral. Nervous indigestion I put it down to, or perhaps the pie was a bit off. Anyway, Anthony was here and Macintosh wrote out a prescription for him to take down to the chemist as soon as they opened, but it sounded like the same mixture as he'd ordered for Dolly, so I told him to tear it up. I was glad I had too, because I felt better as the day went on and I was able to swallow a cup of soup at dinner time. But I wanted to be sure it wouldn't churn things up again, so I got this bottle out of the medicine chest and gave myself a couple of spoonfuls. Next thing was I had this fiendish attack and it was while that was going on that I remembered what Dolly had told me about the medicine. That's why I want you to find out whether there's anything wrong with it.'

'Okay, I'll do my best, but I should warn you that it may take three or four days. Robin's had to go to Manchester and I shan't see him until tomorrow evening.'

'Doesn't matter. No special hurry.'

'And now that we've settled that, are you going to read your letter?'

'Only if you open it for me. I can never get the hang of those fiddly aerogramme things. Can't think why people bother with them, just to save themselves a ha'penny or two, when they've got as much money as she has. I assume it is from Paula?'

'Yes. Paula Van Kliefen, Johannesburg.'

'Go on, then, open it up!'

I invariably have difficulty with the fiddly things myself, but managed to make a job of this one and handed him the unblemished page. He then informed me that he was unable to read it without his glasses and couldn't remember where he had put them.

'No, no, don't bother,' he snapped, as I stood up with a martyred look on my face. 'Read it aloud to me! I suppose you can manage that?'

'Willingly,' I replied and began to do so.

However, I had got no further than *Dear Uncle Philip* and had it explained to me that Paula, who had been nine years old when her father re-married, had been encouraged to address her stepmother as 'Auntie Dolly', hence his status as honorary uncle, when the telephone rang. Before I could reach it the call had been taken by someone on another extension and I heard a man's voice say: '. . .you'll get a highly coloured version in the evening papers, so you may as well hear . . .'

I shook my head at Philip and was on the point of replacing the receiver, but he flapped one hand and cocked the other to his ear, indicating that I was to remain at my post and I then heard Oliver say: '. . . did this happen?' to which the first voice, which I now recognised as Benjie's, replied: 'We don't know exactly. He was found by one of the gardeners about an hour ago, down by the lake. The actual time doesn't seem to have much importance.'

'No, of course not. How utterly appalling, Ben! What can one say? Have you any idea at all why . . .'

'Yes, I regret to say I have. It's been boiling up for some weeks. We'd been hoping it wouldn't come out, but of course there's no chance of that now. It's very bad news, but you'd better hear the whole of it.'

So I clung on and heard it too. It lasted for another three or four minutes and towards the end, despite having covered the mouthpiece, I found myself holding my breath, lest gasps or squeals of astonishment should give my presence away.

'Very bad news is the only way to describe it,' I told Philip when it was over. 'I think you had better leave it to Oliver to tell you himself, because I have a feeling that he'll be pounding upstairs and tapping on the door at any moment.'

It was the wrong feeling, however, because a full ten

minutes went by, in which nothing happened at all. There was still no sound from below, Oliver's car remained stationary and deserted in the drive and Philip, growing tetchy under this neglect, was complaining that, if somebody didn't soon do something about bringing him some lunch, he would want to know the reason why. So I went downstairs to investigate.

II

Oliver was still in the morning room and appeared to have fainted or fallen asleep. He was seated with his back to me, stretched forward over the desk, with his head almost touching Dolly's ornate brass pen tray. However, he raised it an inch or two when I knocked on the open door and, pressing both hands down on the desk, slowly raised himself upright, picked up a crumpled handkerchief from the blotter and swivelled round to face me.

His eyes were red and blotchy, his whole demeanour quite a shock in fact, for I had not been prepared for his grief for his friend and partner to be so intense. His words, uttered in a hoarse voice, were more unexpected still: 'Ah, Tessa! Just in time for the last obsequies! It's all up with me, I'm sorry to tell you.'

'Why, Oliver? What's happened?'

'Benjie's father has committed suicide.'

'Yes, but . . . No, what am I saying?. . . But how ghastly! When?'

'Early hours of this morning, it seems. Ben has just been on the line. They found him by the lake in the grounds, shot through the head. The gun was beside him.'

'What a dreadful shock! Poor old Benjie! And a shock for you, as well, I can see. Have you any idea why he would have done such a thing? Was he ill?'

142

'Ill? Not as far as I know. Deranged, perhaps, but nothing physical.'

'You sound very sure of that,' I said, feeling that for all my diligence, there must have been something I had missed in my eavesdropping exercise.

'Unfortunately, I am. Benjie didn't actually say so on the telephone, but putting two and two together and adding various bits and pieces I've picked up over the past week or two, I have the distinct impression that, if he hadn't killed himself, he'd have been arrested by this time tomorrow.'

'What for?'

'Oh, fraud . . . misappropriation of funds . . . I don't know all the technical terms.'

'As bad as that? Can it really be so, Oliver? He's always been regarded as one of our more respectable tycoons.'

'So many of them are, aren't they, until they get found out? I can't tell you any details, but it won't be long now before they're public property. Things started to go wrong a few months ago on the stock market, I gather. A take-over bid which fell through, or something of that kind. I'm very ignorant about such matters and he may have been covering up for years, for all I know. I realise now that his wife must have been living in terror of something like this. That's why her nerves had gone to pieces and why Ben felt it necessary to spend so much time with her. They are, were, such a close family, you know.'

'Yes, it must be appalling for them both and I'm deeply sorry, but listen, Oliver, you began by saying that it was all up with you and I can't understand why that should be? Did you mean that you had invested money in one of his companies?'

'God no, nothing so simple. I invested every penny I could lay my hands on in the play and you know how that turned out!'

'You lost the lot, of course, but that's been known before,

143

countless times, in our business and there's nothing disgraceful in it, or final either. You'll soon get on your feet again and find ways to raise some more.'

'I'm not sure I want to. One could hardly call it a happy venture. Besides, you haven't begun to grasp what kind of a mess I'm in. It may be no disgrace, but the fact remains that we're badly in the red. Not due to mismanagement, whatever people may say, but to quite exceptional bad luck. Having to bring in two cast replacements during rehearsals didn't help.'

'And nothing left in the kitty at all?'

'Less than nothing, as it turns out. Our cover against further losses seemed solid enough until half an hour ago. It was in the form of personal guarantees from Sir Joseph, Ben's father, and you can imagine how much they'll be worth now? We'd planned to spend a couple of days sorting everything out and seeing what was the least we needed to get by with, but it would be a waste of time. I'll either have to skip the country before the message gets through to the creditors, or sit back and wait for the blows to start falling. The first alternative seems the most attractive at the moment.'

'I'm sorry, Oliver, I really am. It's rotten for you, but do try not to despair. If I can think of anything constructive which might help, I'll let you know at once, but just now I've got to get a move on. Mrs Gale doesn't come until the afternoon on Thursdays and Philip is bleating about his lunch. I said I'd fix him some scrambled eggs and he'll be banging on the ceiling if he doesn't get them soon. Shall I do some for you, while I'm at it?'

'What? Oh, no thanks, Tessa. You're very kind, but I couldn't face food just now. I'll get something later.'

'Mind you do! And I apologise for pestering you with domestic problems at a time like this, but I have to know. Will you be skipping the country this afternoon, or can you stick around until Philip's on his feet again?'

'I don't know. I seem to be incapable of making decisions at the moment. This news has blotted out everything. Even that tiresome business with the keys seems so trivial by comparison. But yes, now I think of it, I told Benjie he would find me here, if he wanted to get in touch for any reason. I'll stay until tomorrow at any rate.'

'Good! And when you've got yourself together a bit and made some plans, give me a buzz, will you? I'll be staying at Roakes Common tonight, which is not far away, so I could be over here in half an hour, in case of emergency. The number's on the pad by Philip's bed.'

I had much to ruminate on while beating up the eggs and afterwards, during the twenty minutes' drive to Toby's house and one question kept recurring. Should this fresh disaster be seen merely as the latest in the long series of misfortunes which had been raining down on Oliver, or could it conceivably be linked, however remotely, with the murder of Dolly Mickleton?

III

'So you never heard what Paula had to say, after all?'

'Oh yes I did, and with no nudging either. When we realised that Oliver wasn't coming up to break the news in person, Philip asked me to repeat what had been said on the telephone. So I gave him the gist of it, but, as it didn't concern him personally, he wasn't greatly interested. He threw out some remark about how distressed poor Dolly would have been to hear about it, because Lady Hartman had been one of her oldest friends, but I took that to be a passing token to the vanity of the departed. So that didn't take long and then he asked me whether I was, or was not going to read Paula's letter aloud and I said I was and I did.'

'Well, go on! Is she going to renounce the money and hand it back to him?'

'Not on your life! If Philip had any hopes of that kind he

must have been disappointed. Though, to be fair, I didn't get the impression that he had. He agreed with me that she's probably like a good many other well-off people, who believe that either everyone else has just as much money as they do, or that, if not, it's because, for some reason, they prefer to be without it. However, I also suspect that many of them only pretend to believe that because it suits them to and in their innermost souls they are racked with guilt about it at least twice a year. Paula strikes me as belonging to that category.'

'I congratulate you!'

'What for?'

'You appear to have penetrated so deep into her mind, and with only one little air letter to guide you!'

'Well, you see, Toby, in one paragraph she chooses to infer that Dolly had settled a lot of money on Philip before she died, so as to avoid death duties, and that her own paltry share is no more than a drop in Auntie's financial ocean; and in the next it sneaks out that she also feels that some compensation is due to him, with the onus on her to provide it.'

'And how does she resolve this awkward contradiction?'

'She announces that she has received a cable from the solicitors, giving her the bare facts of her inheritance and saying that a copy of the will is on its way to her. However, being the sound little business woman Philip assures me she is, this will not do for her. She is sure there will be endless papers needing her signature and matters to be settled about probate and so forth, and that all this will be a very dragged out business, if it has to be conducted by correspondence. She therefore proposes to come over to England next week and deal with it on the spot. I expect her real purpose is to make sure there is no hanky panky and to put paid to any idea Philip might have about contesting the will.'

'Doesn't sound like much compensation for him in it, so far.'

'No, but here comes the sugar round the pill. She ends by saying that she can't tell how long she will need to spend in

146

London, but that, when she returns to Johannesburg, she would like Philip to accompany her, as she feels it would do him all the good in the world, at this sad period of his life to have a holiday in the sun. She will fix the details with him when she arrives, but in the meantime she is so optimistic about obtaining his consent that she has already made the provisional airline reservations for them both. In other words, making it clear that all expenses will be paid. You see what I mean about the guilty conscience?'

'And how does Philip take to the idea?'

'He is tempted, I am glad to say, as well he might be, because she has thought of everything and forestalled all his objections. For instance, she says there will be no need for him to spend more time than he wishes with her and the boys, since she intends to put what she calls the guest chalet entirely at his disposal. So he will be able to retire from the hurly burly of family life to the privacy of his own apartments whenever he feels inclined to. Personally, I feel grateful to Paula and to Dolly too, for having had the sense to leave everything to her. Philip in England, with heaps of money, would have been an improvement on our present situation. Philip in South Africa will be better still.'

'So you think he means to go?'

'He'd be a fool not to. What can he lose? All the same, cunning and diplomacy will be needed, if we are not to gum things up. He is so pigheaded and perverse that the more we urge him to give it a try, the less inclined he will be to do so. And, if he once gets the idea that we can't wait to go belting down to Heathrow to wave him goodbye, the whole scheme will go straight up the spout.'

'You had better leave it to Paula to get round him. She sounds the sort of woman who knows exactly what she means to do and he will find himself being swept along on the course she has mapped out for him, whether he likes it or not.'

'Yes, I expect you're right. The curious thing is that,

although they weren't related, she and Dolly sound like two of a kind, don't they? I daresay Paula managed to pick up a few tips in her formative years.'

CHAPTER SIXTEEN

'Here you are!' Robin announced two days later. 'You may return it to the owner and tell him to put it back in the medicine chest. That should please him.'

'You mean it's harmless?'

'About as toxic as Milk of Magnesia.'

'What a pity!'

'Is it? Why?'

'Well, you see, if someone had really been putting arsenic in Dolly's indigestion mixture, then perhaps, given time, something else, like another bilious attack, might have sent Philip plunging into a new burst of total recall and he would have been able to remember who it was. But no chance of that, now that we know for certain that it was all in her imagination, just another instance of the hypochondria getting out of control.'

'Anyway, what's it to you? You told me you had renounced all idea of sticking your oar in?'

'Oh, I have. This would have been purely for my own entertainment. And, in my detached way, I cannot help feeling interested, you know. There are so many curious features about this case. Improbable as it may sound, I begin to think it may have been a conspiracy, more than one person involved.'

'Thank you, I do know what a conspiracy is.'

'Okay, if you're so clever, tell me something else. Take the hypothetical case of a celebrated financier, whose empire, unknown to all but a few, is crumbling around him, but who is still fighting to stave off disaster.'

'And, having taken it, what am I supposed to do with it?'

'I would like to know whether it would be possible for who

had got wind of the situation to leak it to the press, thereby making the crash inevitable? Or, to be completely accurate, whether the threat of doing so would carry any weight?'

'I suppose a good deal would depend on which press you had in mind?'

'Oh, is there more than one?'

'In the sense that I do not believe there is an editor in this country who would touch a story like that with asbestos gloves clamped round a barge pole. It would be far too hot a potato. On the other hand, I can see that it might have great appeal for some foreign newspaper, say German or American, where the libel laws are different from ours. Does that answer your question?'

'Yes, thank you.'

'And is your hypothetical financier call Sir Joseph Hartman, by any chance? Just like the real one who shot himself the other day?'

'Yes to that too.'

'But it's all strictly for your own entertainment?'

'Yes, for the third time, although I will admit that it's beginning to get a grip on me.'

'Well, presumably, if there is a link, it will soon be found, but you do seem to have got in ahead of the field, so perhaps it would be worth following up. In the meantime, I have something else on offer for your entertainment this evening. I thought we might take a look at that play you've been talking about. We're supposed to pick up the tickets by seven o'clock, but I can ring up and cancel them, if you're not in the mood for it.'

'The girl's quite good, don't you think?', he asked during the interval, evidently pushed for something to praise.

'Not bad, if you happen to like fat legs and a lot of teeth. Clarrie would have been better.'

'Oh, surely not? This one is meant to be defenceless and

vulnerable, which is hardly how I think of Clarrie.'

'Her character has nothing to do with it. Apart from having the right number of teeth, she is a much better actress.'

'All the same . . .'

'Yes, yes, I know what you mean. She wouldn't really be right for it, I know that. I suppose the truth is that she's on my mind.'

'There now! And here have I been congratulating myself that she was getting off it at last. There's been a merciful silence from that quarter over the past few days.'

'Which is precisely the trouble. I have a nagging suspicion that she may be more defenceless and vulnerable than appearances suggest, or than she is aware of herself. So I worry when I don't hear from her.'

'I can't imagine why. If ever anyone was capable of looking after themselves, I'd have backed her to make a good job of it.'

'I suppose it must be on account of Pete that I feel uneasy. There's something about him I don't trust. She finds his jealousy and mischief-making a huge joke, but in my opinion he could be dangerous.'

'And you may be right there. I know my Superintendent would endorse every word.'

'Is that so? Meaning that Pete is still high on his list?'

'High enough, although it's mainly based on hunch, as far as I know. Or, as some would say, prejudice. That promising line I told you about of the antique business being partly a cover-up turned out to be a dud. Nothing to support it, as yet. That was the second bell, by the way. Shall we go back, or have you had enough?'

'Oh no, let's go back. You never know, it may get better.'

'Were you serious when you advised me to push on?' I asked in the car going home.

'Am I ever not serious?'

'Frequently, and this is such a reversal of the usual line I get from you.'

'I know, but I've been watching you during the rare occasions when you've been at home during the past week and I've seen what I'm up against. You go around like a zombie, with a soppy look on your face, straightening pictures which are straight already and picking things up, so that you can put them down again, and it's clear that your thoughts are miles away.'

'Oh, not all the time!'

'Often enough to show which way the wind is blowing. That's why I got the tickets this evening. I hoped an excursion into the theatre might snap you out of it, bring you back to what you think of as reality. A waste of time, as it turned out. If anything, it made you worse than ever. You hardly referred to the play once, just went on and on about Clarrie.'

'How boring of me!'

'Yes, it was, boring beyond belief. And I think you had better try some other way to get it out of your system.'

'I see! So you are thinking of yourself, as well as me? Well, that's a comfort. At least, I shall get plenty of co-operation.'

'And would you like a piece of practical advice to be going on with?'

'Very much.'

'It hinges on another reason I have for encouraging you to go ahead, which is simply that I see your task this time as a purely mental exercise. Therefore, you will be in less danger of putting yourself at risk, or getting into any really bad scrapes.'

'Why must it be a purely mental exercise?'

'It's in the nature of things. Now that the company is split up, you have no hope of acquiring any more information than you possess already. And you'll achieve nothing by pounding round fabricating excuses to get in touch with them all again and arousing hackles and suspicions by asking awkward questions.'

'So what do you suggest instead?'

'My advice would be to take the telephone off the hook and spend a couple of days writing down everything you can remember about what happened, which could conceivably be relevant, from the moment when the first letter arrived. And I do mean everything; not only events, but people's reactions to them and what they said.'

'It would fill a book.'

'Okay, write a book!'

'Perhaps you are hoping that months before it is finished the murderer will have been caught and brought to trial?'

'Well, that wouldn't be bad, but I am actually quite serious about this. I feel that if only you were to get it all down in the right order, with nothing left out, you might well discover a point where someone had slipped up, revealed more knowledge than an innocent person could have possessed, that kind of thing.'

I was grateful for the advice, which I considered sound enough in its way, so did not spoil it for him by saying that I believed I already had discovered who had slipped up, not once but several times. The snag was that my only hope of proving it lay in pounding round and asking awkward questions.

CHAPTER SEVENTEEN

As so often happens, the one on whose answer most depended was, from the asking point of view, of such supreme awkwardness as to make all the rest seem like child's play. After wasting half an hour trying unsuccessfully to fabricate an excuse, I put it aside, leaving it to chance or the inspiration of the moment to provide one and concentrated instead on those in the easier category. On this list there were one or two names for whom no fabrications were needed, so, having put the telephone back on its hook, I rang up Clarrie and dished out a quantity of jam, before coming to the pill inside it and asking her how Pete was getting on and whether he'd been in any more trouble with the police.

'Not as far as I know,' she replied, 'but then I wouldn't, would I? We're not speaking at the moment.'

'Oh, Clarrie, not another row?'

'But yes, indeed! I can never describe to you how he's behaving.'

'What have you fallen out over this time?'

'Well, like I was telling you, I've been offered this job in Manchester and naturally I want to do it, who wouldn't? It's only six weeks and I shall be working like a packhorse from dawn till dawn, but of course he can't leave London himself and the silly fool has got it into his head that it's only an excuse to get away from him. He's been popping off threats like a machine gun.'

'What kind of threats?'

'When last heard from, they were coming in two varieties. One was to do me a mischief, such as gouging my eyes out, so that I'd keep banging into the flats. The other was to run up to Manchester one afternoon and set fire to the theatre. Talk about tempestuous! Honestly, Tessa, nobody knows what I have to . . .'

She continued in this strain for several more minutes and I knew there was no hope now of getting her to talk of anything but herself, but I wasn't bothered. In a curious way and with hardly any prompting, she had not only swallowed the pill, but handed back some jam as well.

Philip came next on the list and, after the routine enquiries, I told him that his indigestion mixture had been tested and found wanting.

'Wanting?'

'Of contamination.'

'Nothing wrong with it, eh?'

'Nothing.'

'So that's that. The hypochondria must have got a worse hold on her than I'd realised.'

'Not necessarily, Philip.'

'My dear child, you're talking nonsense! If it had got to the pitch of imagining that her medicine was being poisoned, she must have been in a pretty bad state, poor darling.'

'Surely the point to remember, though, is that she was convinced that someone was trying to kill her and, as we know only too well, there was nothing imaginary about that. Hypochondria doesn't enter into it because, naturally, in that situation, she would have become suspicious of everyone around her and everything she touched. If she believed it was the medicine which was making her ill, what more logical than to assume there was something sinister about it?'

'Well, yes, I see what you mean. I hadn't thought of it in quite that way, but I daresay there's something in what you say. Doesn't get us any further though, does it? What you might call a dead end.'

Feeling that he might have found something else to call it, I dropped the subject and made some more enquiries about his own health and well-being.

'Better, as I told you, but not right yet and I get very depressed. It's not much fun being stuck here all on my own, you know. I'm getting absolutely sick of it.'

'I'm sure you are, but perhaps you'll be winging off to Africa quite soon?'

'Oh, I don't know about that, I haven't made up my mind yet. And don't say "Oh Philip!" in that mournful voice.'

'Well, I know it's none of my business and I shan't try and persuade you against your will, but, honestly, wouldn't it be the best thing? You'd be well looked after and not lonely any more and you wouldn't need to stay longer than a month or two, if you found yourself getting bored.'

'A month or two? Whatever gave you the impression that I would dream of staying as long as that? Two or three weeks would be my limit.'

'Oh, but would it be worth the trouble of going all that distance for such a short visit? You'd hardly have got settled in when it was time to come home again.'

'My dear girl, what are you talking about? I have no intention of getting settled in. I do have my living to earn, let me remind you. You seem to forget that I am now virtually penniless.'

'No, I hadn't forgotten, but this holiday won't cost you anything and I should have thought it would be only sensible to take a few months off, after all you've been through.'

'Then you thought wrong. It might be possible, if I were thirty years younger, but no-one of my age could expect to come strolling back after an absence of three or four months. Everyone would have concluded that I was dead by that time. I'd be a write-off.'

I was privately of the opinion that he had become one already, after an absence of only three or four days, but saying so would not have advanced my cause, so I switched to a new

156

tack: 'What does Dr Macintosh think of the idea?'

'Oh, he's like you, all in favour of it. In fact, he's talked me into having those jabs done, vaccination and so forth. No harm in it, I suppose. He tells me that the last lot I had are out of date now and one never knows what may crop up.'

'Are you well enough for that sort of thing?'

'I wouldn't have thought so, but he says there's nothing to it. He's threatened to bring all the stuff round this afternoon and get it over in one go. Everyone seems to be trying to hustle me and I'm getting a bit sick of it.'

Working it out as I went along, I said: 'Well, listen now, Philip, I had thought of looking in on you myself for a few minutes this afternoon, on my way to Toby's, but I don't want to clash with the doctor. Did he tell you what time he'd be coming?'

'Between four and five, he said. Not that you can rely on him, but I know he has to be back for his surgery at five.'

'Oh, that's all right, then. I'll be there before that.'

'Well, don't make it too early. I like to have a rest after lunch.'

'Okay, some time after three. I'll bring your medicine back and, if you want to give me a list of anything urgent you need, I'll see to that too.'

This proved irresistible, as I had known it would, and a note of cordiality crept in, as he informed me that he was getting low on whisky and gin and could do with a bottle of each.

One way and another, he was turning out to be an expensive invalid, but I had hopes of the next outlay proving to be a sound investment.

Oliver, who had been at the top of my list of the easy ones, was proving hardest of all to track down. I had sought to put the wheels in motion on Sunday evening, the day after our jaunt to the theatre, by ringing him at home. He wasn't in, so

I left a message on the answering machine, asking him to call me back, either the same evening or before he left for the office on Monday. Nothing was heard from him until just before lunch, when he explained that he had been unable to comply, having returned home very late the night before and because eight to nine a.m. was jogging time. This came as a big surprise, for panting round the park in a track suit was the last sort of activity I associated with him. It proved once again that there is always something new to be learned about everyone, and so I was not discouraged.

'I do hope it wasn't anything urgent,' he asked, after the usual stream of apologies.

'No, not at all, that's why I didn't interrupt you at work. It was simply to ask if you'd heard any more from your mugger friend?'

'How very thoughtful of you! No, not a word.'

'So, whatever else he was up to, it didn't include black-mail?'

'You think not?'

'If so, he's not being very efficient about it.'

'Perhaps he is biding his time? Well, that suits me. The longer he bides it, the better, as far as I'm concerned.'

'Specially as you now believe you could produce a credible explanation for the keys being in your pocket. He's losing ground every day.'

'Well, that's one way of putting it.'

'So, one way and another, the operation could be said to have misfired?'

'Yes . . . well . . . listen, Tessa, it was sweet of you to ring, but I do . . .'

'Yes, I know, you're busy and I'm holding you up, but before you go, there was one other thing I wanted to ask you. How's Benjie making out?'

'Absolutely shattered, poor fellow.'

'I am sorry!'

'Yes, it's a rotten outlook all round and looks like getting worse.'

'Financially, do you mean?'

'Among other things. They may weather the storm, but I begin to doubt it. Still, it's the old man's death that has been the worst blow and nothing can alter that. Benjie was devoted to his father, you know. He'd have done anything for him, absolutely anything.'

'Yes,' I agreed, 'I am sure he would.'

CHAPTER EIGHTEEN

'Here you are!' I said, handing over the bottles. 'Something to cheer you up! Not that you appear to need it. You're looking better, I'm glad to say. Have you been out yet?'

'No, but I went downstairs for an hour or two this morning.'

'You ought to take a turn in the garden. It's a lovely day and the fresh air would do you good.'

'Thank you, but I can see the lovely day and get all the fresh air I need, sitting by this window.'

'So why bother to go downstairs?'

'Had to. That Superintendent was here again. I didn't want him tramping all over my bedroom.'

'Did he have any news?'

'Oh, he wasn't giving much away. Talked in platitudes, mostly. Things like how they were following up various lines of enquiry and expecting a breakthrough any day now. Lot of guff, if you ask me. I'm getting sick of it.'

'I should think you must be, if he got you all the way downstairs just to tell you that.'

'It wasn't just for that. He'd brought some more questions to badger me with as well.'

'What about?'

'You are an inquisitive girl, aren't you? Always were, I remember.'

'Well, go on! What sort of questions?'

'You'll be surprised when I tell you. Last thing I expected. It was mainly about the charity committee poor Dolly used to sit on. He'd brought a list of the members, if you please, and he wanted to know whether I recognised any of the names.'

'And did you?'

'Did I what?'

'Recognise any of the names?'

'One or two. One in particular. Woman called Lady Hartman.'

'That's Benjie's mother.'

'I know that, my dear. I told you only the other day that she and Dolly were friends.'

'Yes, you did, but . . . I somehow got the idea that you meant more acquaintances than friends.'

'To tell you the truth, I'm not sure how well Dolly knew her, and I told the Superintendent the same thing. We never went to their house and they never came here, but I believe she and Dolly sometimes used to lunch together after the meetings and Dolly used to put in hours of work on their fund-raising stunts, for which Lady Hartman got all the credit. Allowed herself to be used as a dogsbody, if you want it straight; but as I said to him, what the hell's all this got to do with her being murdered?'

'And what was his answer to that?'

'Oh, started piling on the guff again. Something about how they'd more or less eliminated the possibility of its having been unpremeditated. They now think it must have been carefully planned in advance, so they've got to go delving and poking around in her past, to see what they can dig out there. Can't see it doing them much good, can you?'

'It sounds reasonable to me. Did you tell him you were thinking of going to South Africa?'

'It was mentioned in passing. I said it was all in the air. I hadn't made up my mind yet whether I would or not.'

'What was his reaction?'

'Didn't seem particularly interested. Wanted me to let him know, when I'd decided one way or the other, but he'd be in touch anyway.'

'When does Paula arrive?'

'You're wearing me out with all these questions. How would I know? Some time this week, presumably. You read her letter, so you're as well informed as I am about her movements. And why don't you sit down properly, instead of perching on the window sill like that?'

'I've been keeping an eye out for the doctor and there's a car just coming in now, so I expect that's him. I'll go down and let him in. Goodbye Philip. I'll ring you tomorrow or the next day.'

'Oh, goodbye, and thank you for bringing those things. I haven't any cash on me at the moment, but we'll have a settling up one of these days, when I'm feeling better.'

'No hurry,' I assured him. 'It doesn't sound as though you're likely to flee the country without letting us know.'

'How do you do?' I said, walking up to the car. 'You won't remember me, but I'm Tessa Crichton.'

'Yes, I do, you're the niece, aren't you?'

'Cousin.'

'That's right, cousin. And what's Toby up to these days?'

'Usual. Wearing himself to the bone finding excuses for not doing anything.'

'Yes, that sounds like Toby. And how's the old gentleman feeling this afternoon?'

'Not bad. I think you should use your influence to persuade him to go to South Africa.'

'Oh, you do, do you? And here have I been under the impression all these years that I knew what was best for my own patients.'

'You don't agree?'

'I do, as it happens and I've told him so, but that's as far as it'll go. I don't believe in stampeding people of his age into doing things they don't necessarily want to do. He's been through a bad patch and he ought to be allowed to get over it in his own time and his own way.'

162

'That might end with him sitting up in his bedroom, drinking a bottle of whisky a day, until he either fell out of the window or into a stupor.'

He really was the most open-minded and tolerant man ever to have recited the Hypocratic Oath and I could understand why Toby valued him so highly. Instead of telling me where to get off, he responded with as much gravity as if my pronouncement had come from a senior member of his own profession.

'Do you honestly believe there's a danger of that, Tessa?'

'Certainly, I do. I wouldn't have said it otherwise.'

'That surprises me, you know, surprises me quite a lot. From the chats I've been having with him over the past few days, I'd got the impression that his aim was to get back to work as quickly as possible. I'm sure he sees it as the best way of picking up the threads again and putting this wretched business behind him.'

'That may be what he wants, but he's either whistling in the dark, or else he'll be in for a big disappointment. He has a somewhat unrealistic view of his standing in the profession.'

'But he's still quite a name, isn't he?'

'It doesn't mean much to anyone under forty and nothing at all at the box office. But that's not the only problem. The sad truth is that he's no longer very competent, can't always remember his lines and so forth. And the most ironic part of all is that, in trying to console himself for losing Dolly, he'd find that this was where he needed her most.'

'Her moral support, you mean?'

'It was much more than that. For over twenty years she'd been pulling him from in front and pushing from behind, forcing him into regular hours and keeping the drink down to reasonable limits. A kind of female Svengali, in a way and without her he'll be no more use than Trilby when her voice went.'

'Yes, I can see what you're driving at and there may be

163

something in it. No-one could deny that she was a woman of strong character and a mind of her own to match it.'

'At any rate, where Philip's career was concerned.'

'Oh, in every way, I should have said.'

'Except one. You would call hypochondria a form of weakness, wouldn't you?'

'Now, Tessa, you must know better than to suppose you can trap me into betraying confidences about my patients?'

'But she's not your patient any more, is she? So what could it matter? And I don't see it as anything to be ashamed of. I daresay all these forceful people have their Achilles heels and this happened to be hers.'

'I shan't be drawn into an argument about it, but neither do I intend to allow you to go running around spreading nonsense about Achilles heels and suchlike. It wasn't anything of the kind.'

'Oh, really? Well, I was only repeating what I'd heard.'

'Then you'd heard wrong and, when you get the chance, you can do the poor creature a small service by at least putting that record straight. Until almost the end of her life she no more suffered from imaginary illnesses than you do.'

'By which I take you to mean that she was then beginning to develop symptoms of hypochondria?'

'You may take it any way you like, so long as you don't go spreading false rumours. In all the years I was attending her, I never saw a sign of it until those last few weeks and I put it down then, as I do now, to nervous strain. Generally speaking, she was as normal as the next one, but she'd worked herself into a state about something, this play I suppose, and small wonder, if what you tell me is true about her carrying such a heavy share of the load. Stress affects people in all sorts of different ways, you know, and physical symptoms are neither uncommon, nor necessarily imaginary. Do you understand what I'm talking about?'

'Absolutely!'

'Good! Then I'd better go along up and have a word with my patient, otherwise I'll be late for surgery. Give my regards to Toby.'

'I will.'

'And I'll remember what you said about Sir Philip going on this holiday. It's given me a new slant and I'll put in a word when I get the chance.'

He started to walk away towards the house, then stopped and turned round again: 'There wouldn't be anything to prevent his going abroad, I take it? No formalities about having to remain in this country while the investigation is going on?'

'Oh, I shouldn't think so. He might be needed when the trial comes up, but it could be months before they reach that stage. Besides, he'll only be ten or twelve hours away, you know; and in the care of a very competent guardian, I might add. Almost a second Dolly, by the sound of it.'

'Splendid! So much the better! I'll do what I can to head him in the right direction.'

II

Two days later, having infuriated a number of people by leaving the telephone off the hook for hours at a stretch, I had finished writing down every scrap of knowledge I possessed in any way connected with the murder of Dolly Mickleton, and everything had fallen neatly into place. So far as I was concerned, the answer was now clear and unmistakable and so I went for the last time to The Old Rectory.

Philip was seated in his usual chair by the window.

'What have you decided?' I asked him.

'I am not looking forward to it, but I have decided to go. I feel I have rather been pushed into it.'

'Well, cheer up!' I told him, 'because I have come here to rather push you out of it.'

165

'What do you mean? You were the one who went on at me about it most of all.'

'I know, but I've had second thoughts.'

'Why?'

'Because I've now found out who did kill Dolly. Do you want to hear?'

CHAPTER NINETEEN

'Naturally, it was the last thing he wanted,' I added, having reached this point in the narrative, 'but he knew there was no escape. I was relentless, just as he had been. Ruthless and relentless.'

Two more days had gone by and Robin and I were spending the weekend with Toby, who, unlike Robin, was hearing the story for the first time and who now said: 'I agree. It is the only way to describe him, but what does surprise me is that he should have had the nerve and cunning to devise such a scheme, let alone carry it out. How we misjudged him!'

'No, I feel sure his accomplice must take most of the credit for that. Philip would never have been able to handle it on his own. However, to be fair, he did prove himself to be a far more accomplished actor than any of us had realised.'

'Although, when it came to the climax, his performance fell to pieces, I take it? He broke down and confessed all?'

'In the end he did. At first, he tried to bluster his way out of it. Told me I didn't know what I was talking about and ought to try minding my own business, for once in my life. When that didn't work he changed the tune to a whine and said he'd tell me the whole story, if I swore on my word of honour never to repeat it to anyone. I said what would be the use of that, since, apart from some minor details, I already knew the whole story? Furthermore, as there was no guarantee that I'd keep my word, he would never feel safe, so long as I was alive. I also warned him that there would be no point in trying to overcome that problem by killing me because I had written it all down, which, thanks to Robin, was perfectly true, and put it in a sealed envelope, to be opened in the event of my death. I also warned him that, unlike the anonymous letters, it was locked up in a place which he had no hope of finding.'

'So it was he who removed the letters from Dolly's safe?'

'Oh yes. Not that he was afraid of their revealing any link with himself, because everything he told me about Dolly having written them herself and her reason for doing so was true. So he knew they could do nothing to incriminate him, but at that time he had high hopes of the murder being seen as a mindless, haphazard crime, committed by some Jack-the-Ripper type, or else by a burglar who had broken into the flat, believing the owners to be out. The letters pointed away from that theory, so once she was dead the first job was to remove and destroy them.'

'Did Dolly know who her enemy was?'

'She may have guessed, or, at any rate, included him among the possibilities. The step she took to safeguard herself almost proved that she had.'

'Which step?'

'She told Philip that she had torn up the will she had made when they married, in which everything had been left to him. She then revived her former one, whereby every penny went back to her first husband's family again and placed it in the safe keeping of her solicitor. She probably saw that as the best deterrent of all against any plan he might have for hastening her death.'

'I have to say that it would have deterred me.'

'That's because, as I'm always telling you, Toby, you have such a nice, simple, honest and straightforward mind. Having married Dolly in the first place and put up with her for all those years, you would doubtless have settled for continuing to do so, however jealous and domineering she became, sooner than face a lonely and poverty-stricken old age; but, from Philip's point of view, she had played straight into his hands. She had not only removed the last and most dangerous obstacle, she had made it possible for him to murder her with

168

impunity and to keep the money as well.'

'Can you follow this rigmarole, Robin?'

'Yes, but I think you had better leave it to Tessa to do the explaining. Something tells me she is going to, anyway, so you may as well hear it once, instead of twice.'

'That is very true!'

'Let me try to make it easier for you,' I said, 'by sketching in some of the background, and the first point to remember is that, although the murder itself was swift and violent, the planning that had gone into it beforehand and the wall of falsehood which was constructed round it afterwards were the reverse of that. It had started weeks earlier, you see, with Philip systematically building up his own defence in advance.'

'With his now celebrated act of rushing headlong into senility, I suppose you are going to say? Such a wobbly old party that he could scarcely climb the stairs without help, so that when the time came no-one would believe he'd had the strength to tie the knot tight enough?'

'Right! And you may also remember my telling you how dismayed we all were to discover how much he had aged. It seemed like madness to have offered him the part, in his condition. But, in fact, it was only after the contract was signed that the deterioration set in. So that was the ground-work and he gave an admirably sustained performance, never allowing the mask to slip in public for a moment and growing visibly more dependent every day on Dolly. However, in my opinion, the timing was the really clever stroke. There was true artistry in that.'

'I didn't notice anything particularly artistic about it.'

'But can't you see how effectively it helped to divert suspicion away from him? There he was, after years on the edge of the wilderness, poised for a brilliant come-back, the leading role in a new West End production, no less. So, if he had been planning to kill his wife, how could he have elected to do so just twenty-four hours before the opening night, he who had so much to lose by the disruption and postponement which would inevitably follow? Surely, it would be argued, he would have waited until the play had either flopped, or settled down into a comfortable run? All this, plus the fact that he no longer benefited financially from her death should have been, and very nearly was, enough to clinch his innocence. As a matter of fact, he didn't give a damn about what happened to the play, or Oliver's chances, or any of the rest of us, come to that, which is the chief reason why I have so few regrets. You see, he'd already set up a cosy retirement for himself, which was all that mattered to him, although one can't help feeling a sneaking admiration, as well. The choice of that particular time hadn't been on the original agenda, which makes it even more impressive. There'd been a previous attempt, which failed. However, that's part of two other stories.'

'In which order do we get them?'

'I don't know yet. They have their place later in the story, but first we come to those wheels which couldn't be set in motion until after Dolly was dead, in other words the fabrication of false evidence. It came in two separate packages and Philip started emptying out the first one before the crime was discovered. He also managed, incidentally, by a series of small manoeuvres, to delay its discovery by an extra hour or two, thus making it that much more difficult to establish the exact time of death. But his main object in coming along to my room that evening, ostensibly to ask if we'd seen Dolly, was to get it through to us that she never came to the theatre with him on such occasions. She dropped him off there and came back to collect him just before the curtain. I don't know whether I was the only one to find that incongruous. You might have thought it would be the one time when her presence would be most essential. Furthermore, it was a break in the normal routine which had certainly never been mentioned in my hearing and, stranger still, neither Oliver not Pete knew about it. I ought to have realised at once that Pete, in particular, who was always so well informed about her movements, would be in the know, would have made it his business in fact, to check on it, since he was planning to go to the flat at nine o'clock for a short burst of safe-breaking.'

'And Oliver too, as you rightly point out, would presumably have made a few enquiries on the subject before setting forth on a similar errand. I am disappointed in Oliver, you know. I had quite set my heart on him for the villain of the piece.'

'Oh no, Toby, far too vacillating and irresolute. He might have longed to murder her, probably did, but when it came to the point he would never have had the guts.'

'But how about all those quaint stories he kept unfolding to you?'

'Yes, I know, they did take a bit of swallowing, and at one point I got hooked on the idea that he and Benjie were working as a team, covering up for each other, because Dolly had caught a whiff of Sir Joseph's impending collapse and was threatening to spread it around, if Oliver didn't do her bidding. That would have meant ruin for both of them, so it wasn't a bad motive in its way, but what one has to remember about Oliver is that he may be wet, but he's not dishonest. With the exception of his first version of the fake burglary, when he was in a state of shock, every one of those quaint stories was true.'

'There now! And who was the joker who took the keys off him?

'Can't you guess? You know how neurotically jealous Pete is and how wide and deep the chip on his shoulder. He had a kind of fixation about Oliver, who was exactly the type to bring out the worst of his inferiority complex and who had once had a minor fling with Clarrie and still brought her roses. As a matter of fact, Benjie was working up to becoming a far more serious contender, but Pete didn't know that and not being invited to Oliver's party was the last straw. He was convinced that it was part of a plot to break things up between him and Clarrie. So when he'd been brooding about it for several hours in his dreary little cottage, he jumped in the car, drove up to London and parked it in Oliver's court-yard. As far as I can make out, the intention was to burst into the house, hold up the party and more or less drag Clarrie away by force, but before he could get started on this programme the front door opened and Oliver and I came out.

'He guessed we were on our way to find a taxi and that therefore Oliver would shortly be returning on his own and this gave him an idea for an even more amusing form of revenge. He left the car and positioned himself in the shadow of the wall beside the archway and when Oliver came through he sprang on him from behind, pinioned him face down on the ground and went through his pockets. He's very deft and co-ordinated, as you know and the entire operation only took a few seconds. He has a delicate touch too and Oliver was scarcely hurt at all, just a few minor scratches and bruises, but he was scared out of his mind and trembling like a jelly, which was exactly what Pete wanted. In fact, the orig-inal idea had been to go back and wait in the car for another ten minutes, while his victim sweated it out and went through the performance of ringing the police and credit card firms and so on. Then he was going to push all the stuff through the letter box and drive away, the cream of the joke being that when the police arrived they'd find a completely unscathed Oliver, with all the stolen goods lying on a mat in the hall. However, as you know, it didn't turn out that way.

'Oliver didn't dare report the loss of the credit cards because it would have required him to inform the police as well, and he couldn't do that in case it should lead to the discovery that he'd been carrying a set of Philip's keys around with him, and it was this discovery which caused Pete to think again. He went through the haul to while away the time, and he recog-nised the keys straight off, for the best of reasons. So this required thought, but he dared not hang about in the yard, so long as there was a chance of the police turning up, so he whizzed off, parked the car in its usual place near the shop and dossed down for the night on an antique four-poster bed.'

'Came the dawn and . . .'

'And he'd devised a new plan. He realised that there was unlikely to be an innocent explanation for the keys being in Oliver's pocket, but at the same time he was the last man on earth to co-operate with the police or turn someone in. On the other hand, his prejudice against Oliver was almost as rampant and he had no intention of letting him off the hook by meekly handing back the evidence. He decided to return to Martingale Close, push everything through the letter box, with the exception of the keys, Oliver's own, as well as the Mickletons' meaning to hang on to these until he'd found a really clever use for them. He fancied this would give him a strange and demonic power over his enemy, as indeed it did. However, by one of those coincidences with which life is so chock-a-block, he had no sooner arrived and started reconnoitring the surroundings than out steps Oliver once again, this time on his way to collect the Sunday papers. It was a sight which produced in Pete an irresistible urge to give the knife another twist in the wound and within seconds he was inside the house, planting his new tease. You know what followed from that.'

'Yes, he's a right bundle of mischief, isn't he? Did he tell you all this himself?'

'Clarrie and I got it out of him between us. It wasn't too difficult because it was exactly the sort of cruel game which needed someone of Pete's temperament and physique to carry out successfully and, as far as I was concerned, he might just as well have put his signature on the note he left in the type-writer. Also I have to confess that I did inject a hint or two that I was better informed about his early career than he might suppose and wasn't above using a modicum of blackmail

173

myself, should the need arise.'

'Yes, you would stoop to anything, I daresay. What was in Philip's second packet?'

'What? Oh yes, that one was filled with all the rot about Dolly's hypochondria. It struck me at the time as being out of character, but he edged it in so cleverly, not giving it any emphasis or elaboration, but as though stating a well-known fact. As there seemed no point in inventing it, I assumed it was true. The rather subtle part was the way he conned me into getting that indigestion mixture analysed.'

'I am afraid you have overtaken me now because I still don't see what point there was in inventing it.'

'I wouldn't expect you to and it didn't begin to get through to me until after Paula's letter arrived and things had started falling into place. In a sense, I did it by starting at the end and working backwards. How would it be, I asked myself, if he and Paula had organised the murder as a team? And straight-away came the answer to one bothersome question: why did Philip take it so calmly when he was told about Dolly's will? I realised that, if he had murdered her, he would have to put on a show of not being shocked or disappointed, since ignorance of its terms would still have left his motive intact, but he didn't get it right. Either overplayed, or underplayed perhaps, and some intuition told me that he genuinely was satisfied with the way things had turned out. This gave me an idea about the hypochondria, which also seemed to make sense, but the trouble there was that I could only verify it by prising some information out of your friend, Dr Macintosh, and I couldn't see any way of getting round him to part with it. However, the chance to give it a try more or less fell into my lap and when it came to the point it wasn't so tricky as I'd anticipated. I have sometimes found that you can get people to give things away, which they hadn't meant to tell you, simply by stating the reverse of what you believe to be true and so provoking them into contradicting you. It worked this time and he made it clear that Dolly had shown no sign of contracting imaginary illnesses until almost the end of her life.'

'And what was so thrilling about that?'

'It supported my theory that there'd been an earlier attempt to murder her and that Philip had muffed it. Following Paula's directions and using drugs supplied by her and therefore untraceable in this country, he first induced a hefty bilious attack and followed it up by substituting very strong barbiturates for the pills Dr Macintosh had prescribed. It should have been lethal, but he had either misunderstood the instructions, or else she was a lot stronger than either of them had bargained for. Anyway, the only result was that she became even more violently sick and started bleating that it was the medicine which was causing it. So that called for a quick switch of plan and the birth of the myth about her hypochondria, just in case someone were to remember the incident when she later died, either in a way which had been set up to look like suicide, or in the fashion which they eventually settled for. He started putting it around for all he was worth that it had been purely in her imagination.'

'I wouldn't have credited him with enough imagination of his own.'

'Well, as I told you, most of the credit should probably go to Paula, sending out her instructions from Johannesburg. I don't doubt that Philip was on the line to her within hours of the murder being committed.'

'Using our telephone too,' Robin pointed out, 'which makes it so much more depressing.'

'Well, at least one good thing came out of it,' I reminded him. 'When it came to his turn, Philip had had enough experience to make a tidy job of it. After my talk with him the day before yesterday he made no mistake; just the right quantity of pills washed down with the right amount of gin.'

'Yes, I am sure Robin will be grateful for that,' Toby agreed. 'It will save those people he works for no end of trouble and taxpayers' money.'

'So there you have it!' I said, rushing in before my beloved could remind me that it was also our gin. 'I think that's the lot. Any questions?'

'Just one,' he replied. 'I had meant to ask it after you finished telling me all this last night, but I had become rather fatigued by then.'

'Oh, really? I trust you have stood up to it better, Toby? What question?'

'What was Paula aiming to get out of it? Apart from money, which she didn't need? You can't be suggesting that she had hopes of marrying Philip herself?'

'Shouldn't wonder. She probably started the affair as a way of getting her own back on the wicked stepmother, whom she'd detested ever since Dolly first snatched her father away and then drove him to suicide. And you'd be surprised by the number of women who found Philip attractive, even in his dotage. Besides, Paula's probably just as snobby and pretentious as her stepmother and Philip's reputation in South Africa is much higher than it ever was here; less competition, for one thing. Any further questions?'

'Just one, I think, but it's a tough one. How did they manage to communicate? You always told me that Dolly kept him under lock and key, even opened his letters.'

'Ah, but he and Paula had no need to communicate by letter. They had a far more convenient arrangement. Paula kept a furnished flat in London. She used to buzz over three or four times a year.'

'You amaze me!' Toby said. 'And aren't you sorry now, Robin, that you didn't make the effort to get the answer last night? It would have been the very thing to revive you. Where was this flat, Tessa?'

'In Upper St Martin's Lane, curiously enough. Just two minutes walk from the celebrated club which is frequented by so many of our distinguished writers and actors. At any rate, that's what they tell their wives.'